Kern

The Puzzle Quests:

Shimmer's Eggs

Also by Janine De Tillio Cammarata

FIANNA CYCLE

Warriors Within

Eyes of the Goddess

NON-FICTION

What Makes Them Amazing:
Inspiring Stories of Young Adults Fighting Cancer

The Puzzle Quests:
Shimmer's Eggs

By

Janine De Tillio Cammarata

First Edition
Rexford, New York
2017

The Puzzle Quests: Shimmer's Eggs
Highland Mountain Publishing
PO Box 217, Rexford, NY 12148
www.janinedetilliocammarata

Library of Congress Control Number: 2017909410
ISBN: 978-0-9776912-3-4

Printed by The Troy Book Makers, Troy, NY
www.thetroybookmakers.com

Cover Art and Book Design by Carol Coogan
www.carolcoogandesign.com

Printed in the United States of America

Dedication

To my adventurous son, Nick.
Not a day goes by that I don't miss you.
Thank you for opening my heart to possibilities.

To Stephen, Tyler, and Emily. The memories
you all created will last a lifetime.

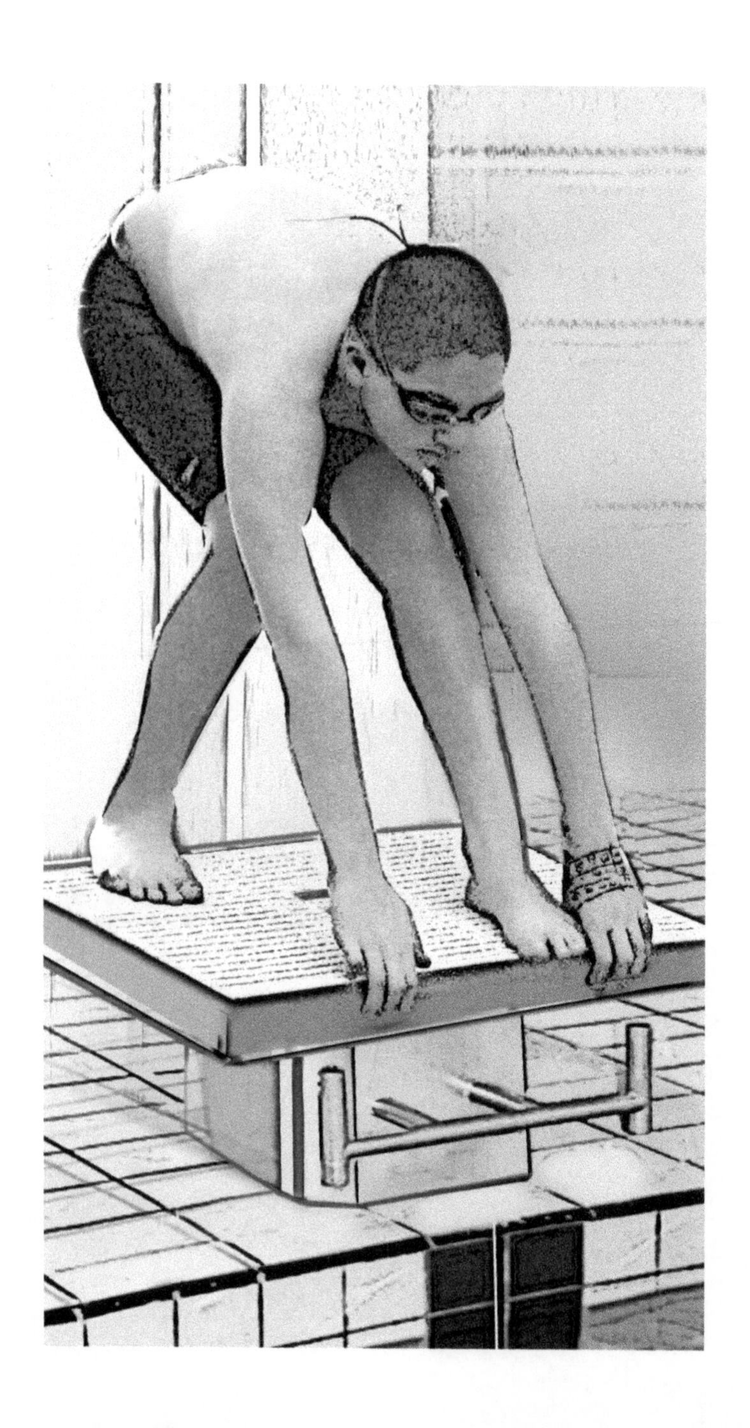

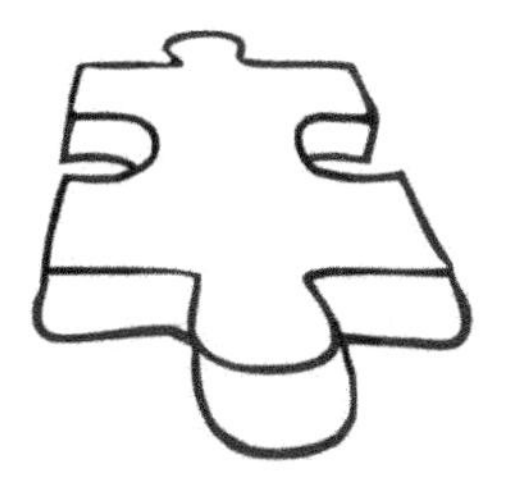

Chapter One

Luke's head spun as he leaned over the starting block. He ignored the pounding pressure. He didn't have time for another painful ear infections or how tired he felt. His team was counting on him to qualify for states in the 11-year-old division, and Luke didn't want to let them down. All he had to do was swim 50 yards faster than anyone else. Luke tried to focus on the water, but the ache in his head distracted him. He squinted his eyes and took a deep breath. When the horn blew, Luke dove cleanly into the pool. He whipped across, his arms lifting, his hands slicing into the water, propelling him forward like a dolphin. At the other end his flip was crisp and his opponents hadn't turned yet. This could be big.

Looking up at the scoreboard just as his hand touched the edge of the pool, Luke let out a hoot. His best time ever. He hopped out of the pool and turned to watch the rest of the swimmers do the butterfly stroke. Luke dropped his head to his chest.

His teammate ran toward him waving her arms in the air. Rose yelled, "You did free style, Luke!"

Despite water dripping in his eyes and the quiet that had

descended on the crowd, Luke shrugged and gave Rose his bright smile. "I'm sorry, Rose. I don't know what happened. I didn't mean to do the wrong stroke."

"But you're disqualified! How can you be smiling?"

Luke looked into the stands and saw his parents and little brother, Peter, watching him. His mom looked concerned, like she knew how much pain he was in. He felt better knowing they were there. That was all that mattered. Luke took the towel Rose handed him. He didn't care that it had the Little Mermaid lounging on a rock staring toward land. He wiped his head and face. Wrapping it around his shoulder, he said, "There's always next time."

Rose could only stare into Luke's brown eyes, his long eyelashes stuck together with water. He laughed and put his arm around his little brother's best friend. "Now it's your chance to qualify."

His coach approached and, wrapping his arm around Luke's shoulder, spoke softly in his ear. Luke nodded. His coach could have yelled at him and said how disappointed he was that Luke screwed up. He didn't. His concern was about Luke's health. Luke was sad he let his team down, but he would try even harder next time.

The following day Luke couldn't swim at the town pool with Mark, his best friend, Peter, and Rose. Instead, he sat at the edge of the diving pool and rated their jumps.

Peter did his best to jump as far out from the diving board to splash his brother with cannon balls. They all had been taking swimming lessons since they were three years old, so Peter easily swam to the edge. When Peter peered over at his big brother, Luke gave him the thumbs up sign and flashed five fingers twice.

Pumping his arm in the air, Peter exclaimed, "Yes!" and ran back to the board to do it all over again.

Luke shook his head laughing. His little brother was such a goof ball. Rubbing his ear, Luke noticed a rash all over his arms. Now what? Wasn't it bad enough he couldn't swim because of his ears? That couldn't be good. Rose did a pencil dive all the way to the bottom of the pool. Luke sighed. All he wanted to do was get back in the water. Swimming made him happy. He was glad his mom had forced him to choose a sport instead of sitting and playing video games all day. Between gaming, building Legos, and reading, Luke had sat around a lot. But now he swam on a team during the summer and another during school, and he couldn't imagine being anywhere else. Luke waved to Peter and Rose, who jumped off the board at the same time to the roar of the lifeguard. Those two were trouble together.

Luke stood, ready to go home. Something didn't feel right.

As he walked toward his mom, Mark called, "Hey, Luke, wait up!" Luke turned, and Mark stopped short. "Are you all right?"

Luke shrugged, "Not really. I have a rash on my arms. I was going to tell my mom."

Mark's vibrant blue eyes widened with worry. "Yeah, well it's on your face, too."

Luke touched his cheek, and it felt hot. "What is wrong with me? I'll miss too many meets if this keeps going on."

"Your mom will figure it out. Don't worry," Mark said walking next to his friend.

Rose and Mark's mom kept Peter with them at the pool while Luke's mom took him to his doctor. They took some blood, and Luke went home to rest.

The next morning, the doctor called and wanted Luke to go to the hospital right away. There was something wrong with his blood. Luke didn't know it, but his whole life was about to change.

After five days stuck in the hospital, Luke was ready for an adventure. He only wished his body would agree. Waking up from a nap, he noticed a gift bag next to him. Peter walked in, pointed to the bag, and asked, "Hey, Luke! What's that?"

Luke shifted his thinned body into a seated position and said, "I don't know. It was here when I woke up."

Peter sat on the side of the bed and placed it on Luke's lap. "Open it."

Luke untied the bow and pulled out a box. "It's a puzzle!" Peter said and removed the cover. Putting puzzles together wasn't anything new for them. It was a family tradition that had started when their mom broke her leg as a kid. She always waited until her father came home to place the last piece since he was often away for work. That tradition continued, except now that their Poppa had passed, the boys' parents placed the last piece.

Luke's face lit up. "Let's put it together." The puzzle was of a dark-haired medieval princess in a long gown reading a book. She sat on a stone bench outside a castle. A shimmering golden dragon leaned over the princess' shoulder listening intently while its tail curled around the bench in a protective gesture. They just finished the border when their parents came into the room.

"Where did you get the puzzle?" their mom asked kissing both her boys.

"It was here when Luke woke up," Peter said. "Do you

know who gave it to him?"

"I don't. Must be a special angel," she said, while studying Luke's tired face. "Dad and I haven't eaten. We can get something and bring it back. What would you both like?"

"We're not hungry. Go ahead and spend some time together. We want to finish the puzzle," Luke said.

After their mom promised to eat and then bring food back for them, the brothers worked while the movie *A Knight's Tale* played on the TV. Luke loved knights and castles and this movie was one of his favorites, because the champion worked hard for what he believed in, never gave up, and won the girl in the end. Peter picked up the last piece and looked at his brother across the bed. Luke was pale and his once broad shoulders had lost a lot of his swimmer's muscle. He had been in and out of the hospital all summer. A frown formed on Peter's face.

"Peter, put in the last piece."

"What about Mom and Dad? We don't want to break the tradition. It might be bad luck."

"We make our own luck." Luke nodded to go ahead, even as his eyelids began to close.

As Peter placed the last piece, a mist formed over the puzzle. Peter blinked his eyes really fast thinking that maybe he was fainting, but the mist grew thicker. "Luke," Peter choked out his brother's name, sounding like he did when he had a nightmare and his big brother was the only one who could chase the scary images away.

Luke opened one eyelid. "What?"

"Look."

As Luke opened both eyes, the dragon shifted its tail and blew smoke out of its nostrils. It peered around and then soared into the air zooming around the boys' heads. It was the size of a mini-airplane and its flapping wings sounded like a mosquito buzzing around their ears.

"Whoa!!" Peter yelled as he flipped off the bed and waved his hands over his head. "What's happening?"

Luke shoved the hospital tray out of the way and hobbled out of his bed, not certain of what he was seeing.

"Watch your IV lines, Luke!" Peter yelled when Luke bent down to avoid the dragon swooping close to his head. Even though he was much smaller, Peter hurried to his brother and guarded him with a fierce protectiveness. "I'm calling the nurse!"

"Shimmer! Settle!" the miniature princess stood and clapped her hands. The boys hadn't noticed her emerge from the puzzle, but now there was a dark shadow where she and the dragon had been minutes before. She was the size of her picture in the puzzle. Smoothing the heavy layers of her purple gown, she spoke to the boys, "I am Princess Meriwether of Castle Dragonia, and this is my faithful dragon, Shimmer. We have been summoned here to challenge you to a quest. If you accept this challenge and succeed, I will grant you a wish."

Luke scratched his head. If his brother hadn't fallen off the bed and freaked out, Luke would have thought his medicine was making him see things. Being a novice magician, he asked, "How did you step out of the puzzle?"

Meriwether's eyebrows scrunched together. "Of all people, Luke, you should believe in magic."

Luke knew he had a vast imagination, but did he believe in this kind of magic? He pondered this and, as Peter stared in shock at the tiny woman and dragon, asked, "Do we each get a wish?"

"I believe your wishes are the same."

Luke stood, dismay showing on his face. Did she know that he hoped to be healthy enough to start 7th grade with his friends? "How do you know our wishes?"

Meriwether waved her hands in the air and said, "I have been granted the ability to take you to our realm. Do not miss this chance."

Peter looked at his only sibling. "Princess, Luke is sick and I'm only 9, so I'm not sure how much we could do."

Meriwether walked toward Luke and tapped his hand that gripped the tray. When he opened it, she stepped onto his palm. Luke lifted her close to his face. As he stared into her small face, he felt a pull toward this person who traveled from some other time and place to find them. "I would not have been summoned to this place if you could not help us. Would you pass up a wish for anything you desired?"

Peter's hazel eyes grew wide as he begged Luke, "We have to do this! We could wish for you to get better!"

Luke held the princess' gaze and then lowered his hand. "What is the quest?" Luke asked, not getting pulled into the excitement of an adventure, even if that was what he had just been hoping for. Even if that wish could heal him. What would it be like to be able to hang out with his friends without worrying about who had a cold? Luke had brushed off messing up qualifying for the states, but what if that had been the last time he would ever swim?

Meriwether hopped off of Luke's hand and rubbed Shimmer's sparkling scales, her concern switching to her dragon. "Let's just say that it will help Shimmer, who is one of the last of her kind."

Golden tears fell from Shimmer's round green eyes.

Peter didn't care what the quest was. If it helped his brother become healthy, then he would do anything.

"What if our parents come back and we aren't here?" Luke asked.

"I cannot go back without you, and all our lives are now at stake. Besides, staying here will only make it worse for you," Meriwether said, wringing her hands with worry.

When Luke still hesitated, Peter touched his brother's bruise-covered arm and said, "Please, Luke! You keep getting sicker!" Peter hated that he couldn't help his brother. If he had the chance to make a difference, then he would do it.

Luke knew he was very ill, and he thought about all the stories his mom wove for them about magical realms and possibilities. Maybe if they had a real life adventure, they could weave a great story for her. She was always so worried and scared. She tried to hide it, but Luke knew her too well. Besides it was better than sitting here missing his friends and feeling tired.

Luke took a deep breath and stood straighter. "We'll help you. What do we have to do?"

Meriwether tapped her tiny hands together, a smile finally showing on her face. "Excellent! Please kneel so that I may bestow knighthood upon you."

"Peter, can you get my pants?" Luke asked. He pulled on the jeans Peter handed him. He wore a t-shirt that read, 'Home is Where the Pool is.' As he slipped into his basketball sneakers, Luke grabbed his yo-yo, along with a couple quarters and his Swiss Army knife. He slipped his iPhone and charger into his pocket and slowly knelt onto a pillow that Peter had placed on the floor. Meriwether unsheathed her sword and stood in front of Luke. Shimmer landed next to the princess and remained still as Meriwether hopped onto her back. The dragon flew toward Luke's face as Meriwether placed her sword that was the size of a toothpick on one side of his thinning, dark hair and then on the other. Luke bent his head forward and shut his eyes, his long lashes a stark contrast against his pale skin. "Do you swear to be truthful, brave, follow the laws of our land, and honor the dragons above all other creatures in our realm?"

"Yes," Luke spoke in a strong voice.

She flew over to Peter whose dark hair was shaved close to his head. He wiggled while he knelt, but when she asked the same question, he exclaimed, "Of course!"

Meriwether laughed. "By the Order of Dragons I dub thee Sir Luke and Sir Peter. You both may rise. Now hurry."

"How will we get back?" Luke asked.

"Fulfill your oath and then we will talk of coming back," Meriwether said.

Luke hesitated wondering what he had gotten them into. He wanted to back out, but he had given his word and that was something he never broke. Luke nodded and asked Peter, "Do you have your watch and iPhone?"

Peter tapped his pocket and raised his wrist to show Luke his watch. Their dad had given them phones that linked with their watches, so they could text and see one another when Luke was in the hospital.

Meriwether stepped onto the puzzle and Shimmer followed. "Now touch the puzzle and come to my world."

The boys placed their hands on the puzzle and a golden light surrounded them, then their arms. It traveled over their head and when it covered their feet, a bright light consumed them.

"AHHHHHH!" they screamed and landed on a cold stone floor, gripping each other.

Peter laughed, rubbing his butt. "That was intense! You all right, Luke?"

Luke stood and stretched his arms over his head like he was preparing to dive into a pool. The t-shirt that had been big on his sickly frame, now fit like the athlete he had been. Luke flexed his arms. "Check this out, Peter!"

Peter squeezed his brother's bicep. "You look more like yourself! Your face has color, too!"

"Amazing!" Luke said lifting the back of his hand in front of his face. Taking everything in at once, he ran toward an arch that could fit three cars across and yelled, "Wow!"

Luke stood on a stone balcony that looked like a landing strip for a commercial airplane. He and Peter ran to the edge and peered over. The front of the castle faced endless water. To their right stretched land and a thick forest with trees as high as they stood. That was pretty tall considering the castle was on top of a cliff. There were stone houses scattered along the cliff, and they could barely make out fields and farms at the bottom.

"Welcome to Castle Dragonia!" a life-sized Meriwether called from the arch entrance. She still wore her purple gown, and Luke noticed the gold band holding her long black hair from her face. Now he could tell she had blue eyes. Luke figured she wasn't much older than him, but for all he knew, she could be married with kids. Royal children were forced to mature quickly during King Arthur's time. Luke was forced to deal with adult issues due to his illness. Some choices he had to make were hard to wrap his head around. Luckily, he had his parents to help.

Luke shook away his thoughts and focused on being in a real live castle. "This is magnificent!" Luke said stepping into the room. "Are we in medieval times?"

"You are in a time where dragons rule the sky, knights fight for their kingdoms, and kings and queens rule side-by-side," Meriwether explained.

It didn't really explain when they were, Luke thought, but he didn't have time to question her further. Both he and Peter jumped out of the way as Shimmer flew into the room from the very same balcony. Luke knew that the Quetzalcoatl was the largest known flying animal of all time and, although Shimmer was much wider around the middle, she looked just as tall. Luke wasn't scared because her green eyes were kind and a bit sad. Her scales glimmered like sunshine on the water after a rainfall.

Shimmer bent her head in front of Luke's face and snorted a wisp of smoke. Luke coughed and then laughed. "Thanks. Good to see you, too." He reached out and patted Shimmer on top of her head.

"She's awfully big," Peter said, standing behind Luke.

Luke stepped back so Peter stood next to him. The top of Peter's head almost reached his brother's shoulders, and he had to stretch his neck back to get a good look at Shimmer. He wished he hadn't because all he could see was the inside of her nostrils. "Pet her. She won't bite," Luke said.

Peter whispered, "How do you know?"

Meriwether laughed and joined them. "Shimmer will not bite. She is quite friendly." She placed her hand on Shimmer's side and whispered in the dragon's ear. Shimmer turned and the boys hopped out of the way of her long tail. Shimmer gracefully settled in front of a gigantic fireplace that scaled 30 feet to the ceiling.

Luke's eyes followed the length of the stone chimney and stared at the ceiling.

Meriwether tilted her pointy chin toward the ceiling and responded, "Ah yes. It's a lovely sight."

"What is it?" Peter asked as he stared up at the colored

pictures carved into the stone. There was a gold volcano, two golden dragons flying around it, and a castle that may have been the one they were in, as well as other scenes. The ceiling was arched so it was hard to capture all the images at once.

"This depicts the history of the dragons, which we can discuss later." She walked over to Shimmer and placed a hand on the dragon's back. "Shimmer's scales contain magical powers that are only revealed when held. In order to fulfill your quest, you both must choose a scale and gently pull it out." At the boys' shocked faces, she added, "Do not worry. It does not cause her any discomfort."

Luke saw Peter's hesitation and, even though he felt a bit nervous, he understood that this was some kind of test toward getting their wish. Luke asked, "Do you know which scale you want?"

Peter placed his hand on the end of Shimmer's tail and Luke chose one in the middle. "All right. On the count of three. One, two, three!"

Both boys easily pulled out a scale and a new one formed immediately.

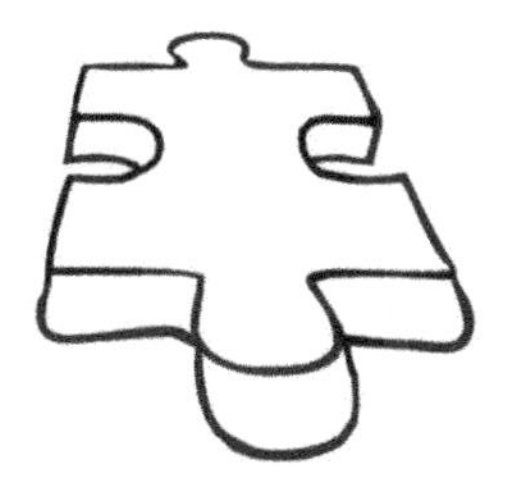

Chapter Two

Meriwether said, "Now close your eyes and think of the dragon. Only then will your powers come forth."

Luke squeezed his eyes shut. Peter closed his and then peeked. The princess watched him, so he quickly shut them again.

Luke opened his eyes and asked Princess Meriwether, "Did you say something? I heard a voice."

"I did not say a word, Sir Luke. What did the voice say?"

"It asked if I was afraid to fly." Luke heard the voice ask, "*Well are you?*" He turned to Shimmer. "Was that you?" Shimmer growled and nodded her head.

Princess Meriwether clapped her delicate hands together and said, "How wonderful! You have been given the gift of dragon speech! That is very rare and helpful for your quest."

"Wow! Hey, Peter, did you hear that?" Luke asked, but Peter still had his eyes closed as he hummed. Luke shook him. "Peter? What are you humming?"

Peter glared at his brother. "What did you do that for? I was humming the baby to sleep."

"What baby?" Meriwether asked, excitement turning her cheeks pink.

"I can sense some kind of baby in trouble." Peter said, his face still scrunched in concentration. Then he looked down at his watch. There was a light blinking on the screen. It was round, and Peter knew that this was part of the quest. They had to find whatever it was. He zoomed in. "My watch is sensing its location, too. It seems to be surrounded by trees."

"That is amazing. We must make quick use of your powers," Meriwether said heading to a wooden box against the far wall that was covered in tapestries. Some showed knights on horses riding into battle. On another dragons flew over the water and sat atop castle towers. Meriwether pulled out two chain mail shirts, which were made of interlocking metal links, two helmets, shields, leg guards, leather boots and gloves. Last she grabbed a sword and a bow with arrows.

Luke's eyes widened. "What does this have to do with our quest and the wishes we get? We have a right to know what we are getting into before we travel out of this castle with weapons."

"I do understand your concern. I shall explain everything once you come back from retrieving the egg."

"Ah ha! It's an egg!" Peter said, thinking he outfoxed the princess.

Meriwether smiled. "Very good, Sir Peter. You are listening. You must rescue this egg. It is one of Shimmer's that has been lost." She handed them their gear. "Put these on for protection. Sir Luke, I believe you know how to use a sword and here is the scabbard to carry it."

Luke took the sword and held it up. He had been taking fencing lessons for four years now and his uncle, who did medieval reenactments at the Renaissance Festival they always attended, had been training Luke to be an actor for their shows. Luke was supposed to play a part in the human chess game, but then became ill. Maybe once he saved this egg, he would feel good enough to do it. He placed the scabbard across his chest and sheathed his sword.

Next, Meriwether handed a wooden bow and a quiver filled with arrows to Peter. One of Peter's fondest memories with his Poppa was learning how to shoot a bow. He had been young, but had taken to it quite naturally and had a good eye. Along with the bow, Peter was a good shot with a BB gun, but he didn't think that weapon would be found in this time. He pulled the string, testing the flexibility of the bow and nodded. "I'm good to go then." He wasn't letting anything get in the way of his wish.

"Peter, place the egg in this pouch as soon as you retrieve it. The pouch will keep the egg warm and secure." Peter took the brown leather pouch from Meriwether's hand and placed it in the front pocket of his jeans.

"Now, follow me." Meriwether wasn't much taller than Luke, but she carried herself like she had the weight of the kingdom on her shoulders. She led them out onto the balcony. "Listen carefully. Shimmer will fly you both to Dragon Forest, since the egg appears to be in there. Peter, it is up to you to listen for the egg and track it. If you are in danger, whistle and Shimmer will help you. As far as I know, Dragon Speech only works when you can see one another."

Both boys nodded.

"Very well. There is one final gift." She reached into a deep pocket of her gown and took out a pouch. She opened it and removed a long crystal tied to a leather strap. She walked over to Luke, and he bowed his head. She placed the white crystal around his neck, which hung below the shark tooth he always wore. "Hide and protect this, Sir Luke. As your time here comes to an end, your crystal will get darker. If you wait until it is black, then you will not be able to go home. The time may vary based on your quest, so you must be diligent and pay attention."

"I didn't realize our quest would take more than one trip," Luke said peering at the crystal, then at Meriwether.

"It may take a few times to get your wish," Meriwether said.

Luke's eyes narrowed at her words. Once again the rules changed. Luke saw the fear and uncertainty on Peter's face. He clenched his fist, but said, "I will make sure we are back in time."

The boys climbed onto Shimmer's back. She ran and then glided off the balcony. She circled back and flew around the castle. Peter was staring up at the sky, but Luke was checking out his surroundings. He could see three large towers with a guard on each. The top was flat and could easily hold a dragon. At the base of the castle was a large dirt area surrounded by stone arches. Beyond, houses were haphazardly placed into the side of the mountain eventually flattening out to farmland. He saw fields of wheat and other grains and vegetables that were too hard to recognize. Beyond the fields were rows and rows of trees. Except for the flap of Shimmer's wings, the wind blocked out any sounds. There wasn't the roar of airplanes or the sound of drivers revving their engines or the intrusion of telephone lines breaking up the beautiful scenery. It was peaceful and simple. Luke sighed and felt like he had come home.

Shimmer landed at the entrance to the forest. The boys clambered off her back. She spoke in Luke's mind. *"This is the furthest I may go. I will wait for you to call me back."* Luke nodded and gave the dragon a pat on her snout.

"That was the most amazing ride ever!" Peter said.

Luke laughed and grabbed his little brother into a headlock. "Yes, it was, but now let's find that egg."

Peter wrestled out of Luke's arm and wanted to continue the tussle, but knew they had a timeline. He'd wrestle Luke when they got home. He couldn't wait. Luke would get better. Peter knew it. They stepped into the forest and onto the path that was marked by 'X's in the trees. The branches of the oak, maple, and pine trees blocked out the sun's rays. The forest was quiet except for the crack of branches under their feet.

"Where are the birds and animals?" Luke whispered.

"I don't know, but it's too dark in here, and I don't like it."

"Use the light on your watch."

They walked on with Peter shining the light into the shadows. The light was strong and lit up the area in front of him.

"Wait," Peter said, grabbing Luke's arm. He turned off the light and checked his GPS tracking the egg. It was close. Peter hummed the melody to *'Ring Around the Rosy.'* "This egg likes that song. He's over there."

They ventured off the path and walked through piles of leaves toward an ancient oak tree. The bark was thickened with age, its center hollow and dark like a deep cave. Peter zoomed in on the tree and picked up his pace. He sang the words to the song and snapped his finger. Without warning Peter was whipped off the ground and hung from a rope wrapped around his leg.

"Help!" Peter yelled.

Luke pulled out his sword to cut the rope when Peter yelled again.

"Monsters! Behind you!"

Luke spun around and with his sword sliced through a stick flying toward his head. Little hairy creatures grunted and swung thick sticks at him. Luke lunged and blocked with his sword.

Peter pulled himself up the rope and untied his foot. He fell on top of a creature. It squealed. Peter screamed and jumped away. It had droopy eyes, big bushy brows, and a bulbous red nose. Another creature scuttled toward Peter, and he flashed his watch light in their eyes. They ran away. "They ran from my light, Luke! They must think I have fire!" Peter called.

Luke was busy fighting off three of the little monsters. "That's . . . great!" Luke grunted. Peter saw his brother was in trouble and jumped in the middle of the fight shining the light at them. One by one they screeched and fled. Peter picked up the arrows that had fallen from his quiver.

Breathing heavy, Luke slapped his brother on the back. "Nice job, Peter."

Peter beamed. "You did great, too! You're definitely ready for the festival." His watch beeped, so Peter walked to the tree. "I'm coming." He moved some leaves and nestled inside the oak tree was a very round blue egg. Peter reached in to touch the egg when Luke pulled him back. Peter fell on his butt and yelled at Luke, "What'd ya do that for?"

Peter didn't listen for Luke's response because the egg's distressful screams were ringing in his ears. Then he clasped his hands over his mouth when he realized that the egg was stuck in a spider's web. A very large web.

"What are we going to do?" Peter whispered.

That was a good question, Luke thought. He could see the bugs rolled up in the web. The egg probably wasn't rolled up because it would have died. A large spider had to be nearby, so they had to act quickly.

"I'm going to cut the web with my sword. You have to

grab that egg as soon as it drops. There's enough dirt that it shouldn't break, but I have a feeling the owner of that web is not going to be happy," Luke said, looking at his brother.

"You want me to put my hand in that?" Peter's face was stuck in a *Home Alone* grimace.

"Yes, I do."

"Why don't you put your hand in, and I'll use the sword."

Luke took a deep breath and let it out. "Peter, Meriwether trusted you with the pouch to gather the egg. You are a knight just as I am. We each have to do our part."

Peter didn't like his brother using the honor code on him, but he shrugged and said, "All right. Let's do this thing."

Luke took a step back so Peter could stand in front of the tree. Leaning over his brother, he cut the bottom of the web. Not waiting to see what might scurry out at them, he cut the top and watched the egg plop onto the ground and roll to the opening.

Peter picked up the egg and hummed to soothe it.

"Put it away and let's get out of here," Luke said, moving away from the tree.

"I will," Peter said as he continued to hum.

Luke rolled his eyes and warily checked their surroundings, nervous that the spider would attack them. Those little guys meant business, and Luke wondered how his wish could come true if he got killed in this place. That thought made him pause. Could he get killed? He would have to think about that and do whatever necessary to protect Peter.

Peter finally placed the egg in the pouch Meriwether gave him. Just then they heard a squealing sound coming from the oak tree. It sounded like a microphone placed too close to a speaker. The two brothers turned to the tree and a pair of red eyes glared at them. They ran out of the forest not waiting to see if the spider was chasing them. Shimmer was nowhere to be seen, so Luke tried to call her in his mind. She didn't come.

"Did you call her?" Peter asked.

"Yeah, but Meriwether said I would have to see her in order for it to work."

"Try whistling."

Luke puckered his lips together and blew. Nothing. Suddenly, they heard loud sounds like tree trunks being ripped out of the ground.

"Luke, didn't Mom teach you how to whistle?"

"Yeah, but I've only been able to do it a few times. She did show me how to use my fingers," Luke said.

The earth began to shake. Luke placed his index and middle fingers in his mouth, pushed the tip of his tongue back, and blew. A tiny sound came out.

"Luke?" Peter whispered shaking his arm.

"Stop, Peter! I can't whistle with you yanking on my arm!" He tried again. The sound was a bit louder.

"Uh, Luke?"

"What?" Luke asked, wiping his hands on his jeans.

Peter pointed. Something on six legs ran toward them. It looked like a bunch of the little hairy creatures all piled high on each other's shoulders, and they were angry. A black spider the size of their Labrador retriever scurried behind it. Peter took out his bow and shot arrows toward the monster. They bounced off like toothpicks.

Luke stuck his fingers in his mouth again and blew. He spit all over his hands, but finally a loud shrill came out as he called to Shimmer in his mind.

Shimmer swooped down, blowing fire toward the creatures. They stopped their chase, but screeched their outrage. She clasped Luke and Peter in her talons and shot into the sky.

"That was close," Luke said.

"We found your egg, Shimmer!" Peter yelled.

Shimmer cooed happily as the boys climbed onto her back. She circled over the forest skimming the highest leaves with her belly and then skyrocketed toward the clear sky. The boys hooted in excitement. They held on tight as Shimmer spiraled toward the castle. She flapped her wings hard to slow down and gently landed on the balcony.

The boys hopped off and ran to Meriwether. Peter opened his pouch and carefully handed the egg to Meriwether, who placed it under Shimmer's belly. Shimmer and her egg curled up contentedly by the fire as the boys told Meriwether about their adventure and fighting the monsters.

"Those are trollics," Meriwether said. Although she tried to smooth the worry from her face, Luke felt her fear. He sat on the edge of a wooden chair and flipped quarters between his fingers. She quickly looked away from him and peered out over the water. When she turned back to them, she was once again the princess who had no choice but to save her kingdom. "There is an evil man named Lord Tam. He must have hidden the egg since it was on his land, but I am not certain. What I do know is that he will use the dragons for his own purpose and that will not be good for us. I have never heard of the large creature or the spider that attacked you. I must think on this, but now you must go back to your world."

Luke stood and pocketed his quarters. "Did we fulfill our quest? Will our wishes be granted?" he said.

Meriwether placed her hands on her hip and said, "Look at your crystal." Luke pulled his crystal out from under his shirt and realized it had turned dark gray. "You must always stay aware of its color for the protection of you and your brother."

"You didn't answer my questions, Meriwether." Luke's glare would have made any other person shrink back.

Meriwether squared her shoulders and said, "There is more than one egg, Sir Luke. You will know if your wish has been granted when you arrive home. If not, I ask that you return and fulfill your oath."

Peter's hazel eyes were wide with worry about getting home and healing Luke. "How will we get back to you?"

Meriwether squeezed his shoulder. "When you get home, take out the last piece of the puzzle. It will lose its magic. Wait two sunsets to let your bodies rest and then replace the piece. Touch the puzzle as you did before. That will bring you back to us. I thank you both for honoring your vows and saving this precious egg." She guided them toward the puzzle. "Now you must go."

Peter hugged Shimmer and then hurried back to the puzzle. Luke walked over to Shimmer and after staring into the dragon's eyes, said, "I'll be back."

"Hey, it's a picture of our house and not the hospital," Peter said as they stared at the wooden puzzle on the table. "Maybe the magic is working!"

Luke smiled at that news.

"Until we meet again, my knights," Meriwether said as the boys touched the puzzle. The golden light encircled them once again.

They were sitting at the table staring at the puzzle when their mother came in from visiting their neighbor. "Wow! You guys are almost done!"

Luke felt a bit dizzy. "When did we get home?"

Concerned, his mom said, "Yesterday. Is something wrong?"

"No, I'm just happy to be here."

She smiled at him and, after she kissed them both on their foreheads, asked, "Where's the last piece?"

Luke hated to lie, but what else could he do? He had to get back to his quest. "It's missing," he said.

"That's too bad," his mother said, with a hint of disappointment.

Peter didn't like any sadness so he said, "The princess and her dragon came alive, and we traveled to their land to help them save Shimmer's egg. We are going back there in two more days."

Luke kicked Peter under the table, but their mom only smiled broader. She pinched Peter's cheek and said, "You never know when magic will find you. I hope you had a great adventure."

"You'll know some day," Luke whispered as he slid the puzzle piece connecting them to another world of possibilities into his pocket.

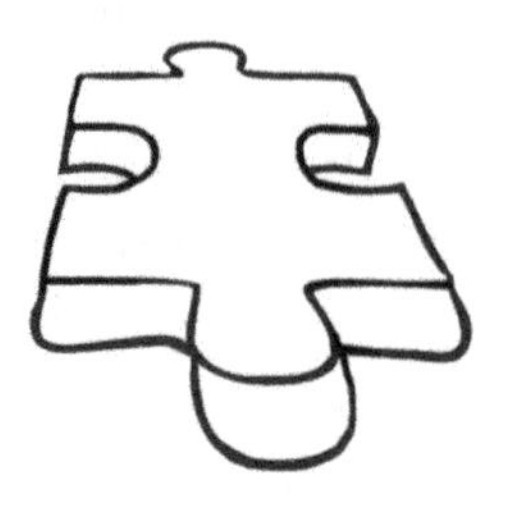

Chapter Three

That Friday the brothers went to their karate class. Peter struggled as he tripped through the movements of the kata he had to learn for his blue belt promotion. It was hard for him to imagine a fight as he moved through the steps. Instead of stepping forward with a punch and kick, he glanced at the clock to see if class was almost over. He poked another student in the back of the head and stepped on his heel.

Luke couldn't laugh because his instructor was focused on him as he messed up his self-defense. He didn't want to be treated any differently even though he could barely keep up, but he would have been hit in the head or stabbed in the gut about ten times at this point. Sick or not, he had to defend himself. Mark lunged toward him with a fake knife and once again Luke wasn't quick enough to step to the side and get out of the way. His mind knew what he wanted to do, but his body was too slow to react. Luke lost his balance and fell over. Instructor Adam was right there and caught Luke before he hit the ground. "You all right?" he asked.

Luke nodded not really embarrassed, just mad that his

body was betraying him. He guessed he didn't get his wish. He remembered the trollics and how he effortlessly deflected their attacks with his sword. He had felt strong. Everything was so much harder here. Instructor Adam always told him to concentrate, focus, and give 100%. Luke thought he did, but he couldn't keep up. Luke sat on the edge of the mat for a bit and thought about the land of Dragonia.

When it was Mark's turn for self-defense, he effortlessly did a backward roll throwing an instructor over his head and jumping up into a fighting stance. Mark had been a wrestler since fourth grade, and it really improved his karate skills. Luke smiled thinking that for Mark the hardest part about wrestling was eating less so he could maintain his weight. Luke had never known someone who loved food so much.

Peter sat next to Rose. He was upset that Luke almost fell, but felt better when Luke gave him one of his trademark smiles. Rose comforted him by placing a hand on his arm. Peter smiled back and couldn't wait to see what their next quest would be. He remembered humming to the one egg and had checked his watch to see if the map of the forest was still there, but it wasn't. He had no proof that he had traveled to another place, and he longed to tell Rose all about it. They had been friends since they were two years old when their brothers had met in preschool. They usually shared everything. Peter knew that Rose would love Meriwether. But he had promised to keep her a secret, and tonight was the night they could revisit Meriwether and Shimmer. It would be tricky because Rose and Mark were coming over for dinner. Finally, class was over and for once both boys bolted out the door.

"See you at your house, guys!" Rose called, but they were already gone.

Mark and Rose arrived at the house about an hour after class. They ran upstairs to the boys' bedrooms, but no one was around. They looked in the spare room where the boys played on their computer and watched movies, but they weren't there.

"Mrs. C.," Rose called. "Do you know where Peter and Luke are?"

"Check in the basement, Rose!"

They raced to the basement. The lights were on and Rose hopped on their oversized camouflage beanbags that the boys sat on to play video games.

Mark took off his satchel that contained all his drawing supplies and placed it on the rug. "Look at this puzzle, Rose," he said.

Rose rolled onto the rug next to her brother and studied the picture. She pushed her shoulder-length blond hair behind her ears. "I love her dress. She looks so real."

A golden light shot out of the puzzle toward their faces. They both fell back and crab walked until they were up against the wall. There was a loud popping noise, and Luke and Peter appeared next to the puzzle just as shocked as their friends were.

"What . . . ?" Mark asked, his clear blue eyes wild with disbelief.

"Oh no!" The boys exclaimed in unison.

"How did you do that?" Rose demanded standing with her hands on her narrow hips.

"I thought time didn't change here," Peter said staring at Luke.

Luke shrugged, knelt down, and removed a piece of the puzzle. The picture lost its glow and so did Luke. He placed the piece in his pocket and took out two marbles. As he twirled them in his hand, he said, "We'll tell you what's going on, but you have to swear not to tell."

"We swear!" They both said at once.

"We've been dying to tell you anyway!" Peter exclaimed and looked around to make sure no adults were lurking on the steps.

"Over here," Luke whispered and the four friends settled down on a green reclining couch in the far corner of the basement. "Well," Luke began, his hands moving in their own language as he rolled the marbles back and forth. "A week ago this puzzle came alive, and we traveled through it to a castle from medieval times like King Arthur."

"With big towers and dragons," Peter said. "Well, at least one right now."

"The girl in the puzzle is a princess called Meriwether, and she needs help with certain quests. In exchange for finishing our quest, we will be granted a wish," Luke said.

"Yeah, the first quest was to find Shimmer's egg. We got to ride on her back, fight trollics, and we are knights!"

Rose laughed out loud in disbelief, even though she had seen them appear out of nowhere. "You just played a trick on us!"

"Then where did the gold light come from?" Luke asked.

"It was probably one of those strobe lights from a prank kit. You are always playing jokes, Luke! Besides, you can't time travel. That's just make-believe."

"Rose, we really went there. Luke was healthy again. You have to believe me!" Peter pleaded.

Rose's face scrunched in disbelief. "What do you mean Luke was healthy?" She glanced at Luke who now was lounging on the couch with the same sickly pallor she had seen in karate class. He had looked like his normal self when she first saw him appear. Why would he feel better there? What did it mean?

"I believe you, Peter," Mark finally said. His wise blue eyes observed them all. He opened his sketchpad. After a few pages of comics and super hero drawings, Mark turned the pad around and showed his friends what he had drawn. In pencil was a drawing of Meriwether reading to a dragon just like the puzzle on the floor.

"Woah," Rose said.

"There's more." When he turned the page, all three kids leaned forward to look at a very intricate map of a forest, lake, cliff, town, and cave. At each location, Mark had drawn an oval.

"What made you draw this?" Luke asked, leaning further over his friend's narrow shoulders. Luke was broader and stood a good head taller than his friend.

"I don't know. I was doodling while eating lunch at camp. Some kids were talking about going to Kines Park to do some BMX riding. I began to draw a path and then another. Each path seemed to lead somewhere. I thought the ovals were stones, but maybe they're eggs."

Luke leaned back and took a deep breath. He rubbed his lower back and ignoring everyone's concerned faces said, "So does that mean the other quests are about finding Shimmer's eggs? I thought they would be different quests, like capturing those trollics we fought."

"And do we have to save all the eggs for our wish to come true?" Peter asked.

"That's a good question," Luke said. "Meriwether has a bad habit of avoiding the answers."

"Maybe Mark is supposed to come with us to help figure out the quest. Maybe he will get a wish, too. That must be why he could see us," Peter offered.

"Hey, what about me? You guys aren't leaving me here!" Rose complained. Rose was petite, but she was very athletic and could keep up with most of the boys in her grade.

"Don't worry, Rose. I think you are part of this," Mark said. He turned a page to show them a comic strip of a girl who, in the first panel, jumped into murky water. In the next scene, she searched for something and sat on the bottom of the lake with gills sticking out of her neck. In the final panel, she held an oval object and swam back to the surface. Mark had titled the comic strip 'Gill Girl.'

"I'm not a fish!"

"No, you're not a fish, but you are the furthest in swimming lessons, and you have been on the swim team for almost a year now. Maybe you will help us on the path to the water," Luke said, attempting to soothe Rose before she exploded at her brother.

"Well, let's do it then!" Rose's attitude changed from mad to determined.

"We can't for two days," Peter said.

"Why not?" Rose threw her hands up in the air.

Luke and Peter looked at each other, and Luke said, "We have to let our bodies rest. Meriwether told us the first time that when we came back we had to take the piece of the puzzle out and not place it back for another two days."

"That'll be Sunday," Mark said. "We need to get together."

"I know," Rose said. "Let's go to the town pool. We can hide in the turtle cave."

"Our moms will notice we are gone," Mark argued.

"Well then we'll have to find a way to distract them. That's usually easy to do."

"The puzzle is covered by a mist and time doesn't move

forward when we are gone. As long as no one sees us reappear, we should be fine," Luke said. "But how are we going to carry the puzzle and put 550 pieces together?"

"Mom has a puzzle carrier that you roll the puzzle into," Peter offered. "I can carry it in my backpack with my towel."

"Sounds like a plan," Mark said, and the kids paired up to compete in ping-pong.

At Dino Road pool, the four friends tossed rings into the pool and jumped in to see who could find the most the fastest. The August sun managed to warm the water. After an hour of searching and playing tag, the kids announced that they were going to have lunch in the turtle cave made of cement. The cave was the hot spot to hang at the pool. It was in the shape of a turtle, but you entered in through the turtle's mouth and there was a big enough opening for four or five friends to sit. Kids had practically covered the inner walls with carvings of their names or initials. Rose and Peter rushed over to get their spot and start on the puzzle. They laid out their towels. Peter said, "I forgot my backpack!" He ran to the other side of the pool. When he came back, Billy Bryce was blocking the entrance to turtle cave. Peter looked around for Rose and realized she was in the cave hiding against the wall.

"Going somewhere, Petey?" Billy asked with his arms crossed over his big chest. Billy was 11 years old, but in Peter and Rose's grade. He was huge and wide for his age. Peter wasn't exactly small, but he had a thin frame from running so much on the soccer field.

"I have my stuff in there, so yeah I'm going into the cave. Please move out of my way," Peter said, but the request came out as a whisper.

Billy pushed Peter, and he fell onto the concrete. He had his backpack on, so it cushioned his fall, but he worried about the puzzle. Peter jumped up, his cheeks bright red with anger and embarrassment. He blinked back tears and thought about what Instructor Adam would want him to do.

Just then Luke appeared and, although Luke kept his smile in place, Peter could tell he was mad. As sick as he was, Luke stood eye-to-eye with Billy and said, "I believe my brother and his friend were here first." Luke nodded toward the opening, and Rose peeked her head out.

"Get lost, Billy! You aren't so tough now that our brothers are here!"

That made Peter wince and his face redder. Mark stood quietly next to Luke, with his hand on his shoulder. Luke wasn't feeling very well and had spent too much time in the sun. He needed to get to Dragonia for energy.

"Whatever," Billy said and shoved past Peter knocking him aside.

Luke looked at his little brother and asked, "You ready for the next quest?"

Peter knew he wasn't like his big brother. He just wished it wasn't so obvious when Billy Bryce was picking on him. He wanted to be the boy who saved Shimmer's eggs, fought trollics, and stood up for Rose. But that was only in the land of Dragonia. Here he was just a 9-year-old boy who got pushed around and thought about what he wanted to say after he was knocked to the ground. Luke said that his courage would come out when he needed it most and that it was harder being brave. Well, hadn't he just needed to be brave? Besides, what did Luke know about it? He was born with courage. Not answering his brother, Peter ducked his head into turtle cave and thought that it was much harder being a coward. He couldn't help it; he was afraid he'd fail in so many ways that truly mattered.

Peter unzipped his bag and carefully pulled out the puzzle that was wrapped in a green felt holder. He opened it on the cold ground and slowly unrolled it. Forgetting about Billy, Peter said, "Hey! The puzzle changed!" Some of the pieces had popped out, but everyone quickly placed them back in. They all kneeled around the puzzle and leaned their heads over it.

"It looks like an arena for training," Luke said. He took the piece out of his bag. "Let's see where this takes us." Luke placed the piece by Shimmer's tail as she flew over the arena. A golden glow encircled the puzzle and Meriwether stretched and looked up.

"Oh!" she said when she saw Mark and Rose. Shimmer flew above their heads and Luke quickly mind-spoke to stay in the cave. They were in a public place and people would see her.

When he repeated it to Meriwether she asked, "Is it dangerous?"

Luke thought about Billy and said, "I don't think so, but it would be hard to explain why a tiny lady from a puzzle is talking and a dragon is flying around." Luke pointed to his friends. "This is Mark and Rose. They found us when we came out of the puzzle the second time."

During that last visit, the boys had spent time in the castle with Meriwether and the villagers. Meriwether had told them that most of the warriors had disappeared with the king and Shimmer's mate, Copper, a few months ago, so the castle was only protected by a handful of knights. Luke practiced sword fighting with other boys his age, while Peter worked on target practice with his bow and arrow.

Luke was so happy that he had energy, he hadn't asked about their next quest.

"We think they are meant to help us," Peter said. "Mark, show her your drawings."

Mark placed his sketchbook on his towel, and Peter turned on the light from his phone. Meriwether was so small it was hard for her to see the whole page. Luke held out his hand, and she stepped on it holding onto his thumb while he lifted her higher.

"Ah," Meriwether said. "I must agree with you, Sir Peter. Have you explained the quest?"

Luke answered, "Yes, to the point that we know, and they are willing to travel with us. We think there is another egg in the water, and Rose is meant to save it. She's a really good swimmer."

"So are you, Luke," Rose said.

"Thanks, but we need you. And Mark is a great artist and seems to know where the eggs are hidden," Luke said. "We want to know if we have to find all the eggs before our wish comes true."

"I thank you for your patience in this quest, and I believe it may be time to tell you more," Meriwether said to Luke and Peter. "Rose and Mark, please kneel so that I may bestow knighthood upon you."

"Oh, Peter! It's like the movie *Camelot* when Kaylee becomes a girl knight!" Rose exclaimed.

"Yeah, you're right!" Peter said. One of Rose and Peter's favorite activities was watching movies together. They usually had a movie night once a month.

Rose knelt next to her brother who was very serious. He put his hand on her arm to still her body as she bounced up and down with excitement. She and Peter were like that—

always full of pent up energy. Luke lifted Meriwether so that she was eye level with Mark. She unsheathed her tiny sword.

She placed the sword on either side of his short dark blond hair. "Do you swear to be truthful, brave, follow the laws of our land, and honor dragons above all other creatures in our realm?"

"Yes, I do, Princess Meriwether," Mark said.

Luke shifted her in front of Rose. Rose's smile was bigger than her face, and her ponytail bobbed up and down as she nodded yes when Meriwether asked her the same question.

"Please rise and, by the Order of Dragons, I pronounce you Sir Mark and Lady Rose."

Rose was the only one able to stand up straight inside the turtle. "I feel taller!" she said.

"What do we do now?" Mark asked with the same stoic face.

Meriwether motioned for them to come closer. They knelt down near her and Shimmer flitted around, but then sat on Luke's shoulder. Luke smiled at her. Shimmer was way better than the fluffy purple puppet dragon that Luke had convinced his mom to get him at the Renaissance festival in the beginning of this summer. Luke could make the dragon move its head while he made noises. But now Luke could talk to a real dragon and even ride it. That made his life awesome and bearable.

"I ask that you come back with me and find the second egg. The other one is thriving and the eggs will hatch in a fortnight. They must not hatch in the hands of an evil lord named Tam."

"What's a fortnight?" Peter asked.

"Two weeks," Luke answered and asked, "Will you tell us more about this evil guy?"

Meriwether's tiny blue eyes beaded with tears. "I will

tell you about him and the rest of the quest, but I would feel safer if we traveled to my realm. The egg is alone. I fear being away for too long."

"All right," Luke said, not wanting anything to happen to the egg.

"Touch the puzzle if you will."

"It's OK," Luke said, as he saw his friends' worried faces. "We'll be right here with you."

Rose grabbed Peter's hand, and he felt braver knowing that he could protect his friend. Together they touched the puzzle. The golden light was dazzling. Peter heard Rose's scream and held onto her even tighter. They all bounced off a packed dirt floor and the light faded. Peter made a mental note to strap a pillow to his butt next time.

"Woah," Rose said. They were in an arena about the size of a football field. It was open to the clear blue sky. Tall rounded arches surrounded three sides of the arena and Shimmer glided through one of the arches and landed near them stirring up clusters of dirt.

Mark coughed and asked, "Where are we?"

When the dust settled again, they could see a long wooden fence set up in the middle of the arena and on one side stood a pole with a piece of wood and a ring hanging from its end. On one end of the arena there were wooden bleachers and on the other two chairs decorated with green fabric perched on a platform. The stone castle loomed tall behind the platform, and Rose couldn't wait to take a tour.

"You are in the knight's training and tournament arena," a full-size Meriwether said as she stepped out of the castle. Her burgundy gown flowed down to cover her pointed shoes and an emerald clasp held her cape around her shoulders. Her black hair flowed down her back in thick waves.

Rose whispered to Peter. "I love Meriwether's hair. I'm going to grow mine out."

"Uh, OK," Peter whispered back, wondering why Rose was so focused on hair when they had dragon eggs to find.

"This is also where the dragons will train," Meriwether explained. "Once the eggs hatch, they will test their wings and become full grown in one month."

"How many eggs are there?" Luke asked, wondering how long their quest would be. School started in a couple weeks, and he wanted to be there.

"Come," she said walking toward the castle. "Let us talk about your quest."

The kids followed with eagerness and excitement. They entered the room where Luke and Peter had first arrived. The egg was in a basket by the blazing fire.

The kids were glad they wore t-shirts and shorts. It was very hot in the room and the temperature outside had to be in the 60's.

"Why is the room so hot?" Rose asked.

Meriwether removed her cape and said, "The eggs must be kept at a certain temperature. That is why I am concerned about their safety. Who knows where the others are and what is happening to them right now." At her words, Shimmer's golden tears fell. Meriwether wiped Shimmer's eyes and said, "Alas, I did not mean to make you sad. We will find your babies. Fret not."

Peter closed his eyes and hummed, *'London Bridge is Falling Down.'*

"What are you doing, Peter?" Rose asked.

Peter opened his eyes and looked at his watch. A dim light showed on the map that only appeared in this land. "The eggs like when I hum to them. It's soothing, but this one," he pointed to his map, "seems to be in an active mood, and I hear gurgling noises."

"Sir Mark, you say you drew a picture of an egg in water?" Meriwether asked.

"Yes," Mark said, and put his satchel on his lap as he sat in an oversized brown chair with wooden dragon claws for feet. He flipped the top to reveal his pencils, erasers, and other art supplies. Mark pulled out his sketchpad and opened it to the rough drawing of the map. "Here it is. There seems to be a stream that leads to a larger body of water. I think it might be a lake, because there are trees and rocks surrounding it."

Meriwether stroked Shimmer on her large iridescent head. "It is time to see what magic is in store for our new knights. Sir Mark, we will begin with you. When Sir Luke was given a scale, his power was the ability to speak with Shimmer through their minds. Sir Peter can sense an egg and locate it on his armband. He is able to communicate with the eggs to soothe them. Now we will find the special magic that is within you."

Mark couldn't imagine what he could give, but pulled out a scale anyway.

"What can you do, Mark?" Rose asked.

"I don't know. I don't feel any different."

"I'm so hungry. I didn't eat before we came," Peter said.

Mark felt his hand twitch. "I need to draw." He sat down on a plush rug and started drawing with his well-loved pencil.

"Can you believe it?" Rose said to Peter. "Mark, you are supposed to find out what your magic is, not draw silly pictures!"

"I know, I know. I'm almost done." When he finished, he held out his sketchpad to Peter. "What do you think?"

Peter's mouth began to water as he looked at the huge hamburger topped with lettuce, tomato, onions, ketchup, and mustard on a Kaiser roll. "That's exactly what I was thinking about eating! I wish it was real!"

The hamburger appeared in Peter's hand, mustard and ketchup dripping down his arm.

"What the . . . ," Luke started.

"All right!" Peter yelled and took a gigantic bite. "It's perfect," he mumbled chewing.

"How . . . how did that happen?" Mark asked Meriwether.

"Magic comes in many forms. It would appear that you have the ability to make your drawings come to life when needed most. It is a wonderful gift and will help us tremendously."

"I want a new bottle of perfume!" Rose said.

"I think the wish must be selfless or at least needed very much in Peter's case," Meriwether said. "Now Lady Rose, let us see what the dragon scale will bestow on you."

Rose thought smelling pretty was important, but she shrugged her shoulders, chose a scale, and gently pulled. The colors sparkled like iridescent blue, pink, and yellow crystals. Rose stared at the scale, willing her gift to come to her. Rose said, "I don't feel anything."

They all waited, but Rose's magical skills weren't obvious.

"Maybe they'll come out when you least expect it," Luke suggested.

"What a rip off!" Rose yelled.

"Lady Rose, I am sure your magical power will be revealed to you. Otherwise you would not have been able to pull out the scale. You must learn patience and wait for the magic to find you," Meriwether said.

"I hate waiting," Rose said and plopped down in a corner.

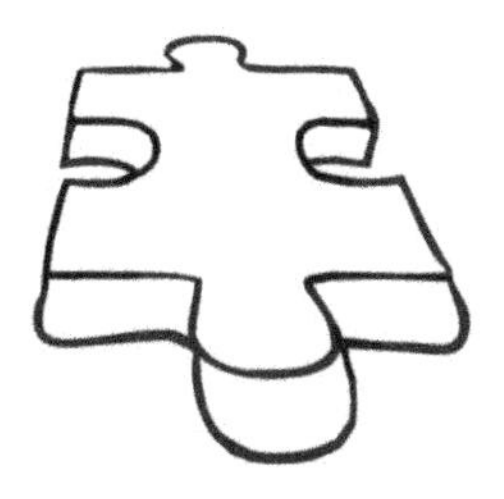

Chapter Four

"Sit so I may tell you about our enemy," Meriwether said. She sat on the green cushioned chair and everyone else settled around Rose who was still upset about not knowing her power. Peter nudged her in the arm to soften her up, but Rose crossed her arms and turned away from him.

"Come on, Rose. Your powers will come out soon. I just know it."

"It's not fair," Rose whispered to him.

"Maybe your power is so great that it will take a while for it to build. I'm sure yours will be the best."

Rose looked at Peter, her blue eyes daring him to make fun of her, but he only smiled. She smiled a little. This time when he nudged her with his elbow, she nudged him back. He did it harder, and she rammed her pointy elbow into his ribs.

"Ow!" Peter said only half serious. Rose laughed, and Peter joined her.

"Knock it off you two," Luke said.

They both made a face at Luke, but turned to Meriwether when she slid off the chair and sat on a burgundy pillow in front of them curling her feet under her dress.

"Lord Tam Brinen lives in the land called Almora which connects on the other side of Crystal Lake. Our families have lived on these lands for generations. We have had squabbles on both sides, but try to keep the peace since there are always enemies attempting to invade our lands. But last year after Tam's father died, he asked for my hand in marriage. It is true that it would have been a perfect union between the families, as well as for protection of our lands."

"Do you love him?" Rose asked.

"Don't interrupt," Mark said.

"It's an important question."

"No, I do not love this man. He is much older, is greedy, and wants what is only best for him. I told this to my father. He and my mother were blessed to marry because of love and wished the same for me. When my father refused Tam, he was very angry and said we would pay for the insult. I guess we have," Meriwether said looking down at her hands. She released the fabric of her dress that she had been squeezing and blinked her eyes to hide her tears. Shimmer growled sadly.

Luke rubbed between the dragon's eyes. Shimmer settled, and they all continued to listen.

"Soon after, my father was attacked while he was away from the castle with Shimmer's mate, Copper, who is an enormous and powerful dragon. My mother, a seasoned warrior, rode her stallion to join my father in battle. Most every knight fought that day. There were many losses. I had just received a message that we were winning, but then no one returned. None of the knights came back, nor my parents or Copper. We have not seen them for two moons now, and I fear that they are gone forever. It is only a matter of time before Tam decides to take my hand by force. We need the dragons to protect us, especially if my parents are gone." This time Meriwether couldn't stop the tears from falling. She turned her head away ashamed that she was not the leader her parents raised her to be.

"Lady Meriwether," Mark began.

She sniffled and asked, "Yes, Sir Mark?"

"How did the eggs get lost?"

Meriwether turned to the group gathered around her. They were her hope to save her family. She didn't understand how they were all connected yet, but she was grateful for their help. She continued. "Dragon eggs are kept with the father for protection and the extra heat allows them to hatch sooner. Since the attack was unexpected, Copper didn't have time to get the eggs back to Shimmer. When he disappeared, Shimmer spent days searching for him and her babies. She could only sense images from Copper's struggle. He must have scattered the eggs around the realm thinking that at least some of them could be recovered, but she hadn't found any until you came."

"That's terrible," Rose said. "What can we do besides find the eggs?"

Meriwether smiled. "Gathering the eggs is a courageous act that will continue the dragon's line. Once the eggs hatch, the dragons are naturally attracted to their parents. This will tell us for certain if Copper is still alive, and perhaps I will be able to find my parents and their knights. As I have said, Tam must not be allowed to take one of the eggs. If they bond, the egg will become evil like him and then we will have dragons fighting each other, which hasn't happened for hundreds of years. What you are doing is more than enough."

Peter fidgeted and raised his hand. "Uh, Meriwether. I

think it's time to go. The egg is whimpering. None of my songs are comforting her anymore, and the light on my watch is fading."

Meriwether stood with purpose. "Very well. You must travel to Crystal Lake. Luke and Peter, you are familiar with some of Dragon Forest where you found the first egg. You will head through the forest and continue until you reach water."

Rose shifted uneasily and scrunched her nose and eyes. Luke could tell she was brimming over with the need to ask a question. "What's up, Rose?" he asked her.

Rose's gaze shifted from Luke to Meriwether. "Well. Why doesn't Meriwether come with us? After all, we are just kids. So is she, but she knows the area."

Mark slapped his forehead in embarrassment.

"That is an excellent question, Lady Rose, and one I should have addressed. There is so much on my mind. As a princess, I am trained in arms and negotiations, but I cannot travel far from my castle. A curse has been placed on me by one of Tam's wizards. If I walk off my land without Tam's permission, I will fall into a deep sleep. The only way I will awaken is if he releases me from the curse. The curse will get weaker as we find more eggs. My freedom is with the dragons and the removal of a chain around Tam's neck that holds a piece of my hair in a locket."

"Is that why Shimmer can't fly us over the forest?" Luke asked.

"No, Shimmer is not cursed like I am, but it is too dangerous. Tam has incredibly large arrows that will pierce through Shimmer's scales and armor. You must hide from him at all costs. Also, half the lake is his, and he guards it with underwater snakes. Be wary of these snakes, for if they grab you, it will be hard to get out of the water."

"And you want me to go in there?" Rose asked, her eyes round with shock and dismay.

"If that is what is required, then yes. Remember your oath to me and believe in the gift of Shimmer's scales. Your power will come when you need it most, but you must have faith that it will come."

Rose didn't know if she believed that magic would happen for her, but she took the oath so that Luke would get better. If she had a chance to help him, she would not let him down.

They went to the balcony where Shimmer waited. As they climbed onto her back and hung on to one another, Shimmer lifted into the air with her large wings. Rose screeched with delight, as Mark held onto his satchel, nervous that it would fall off his shoulder. Shimmer gracefully landed at the edge of Dragon Forest.

"Thanks, Shimmer," Luke mind-spoke. *"We'll meet you back here soon."* Shimmer nodded and flew away. Luke smiled at his brother and their best friends. "Are we ready?"

"I'm ready!" Peter exclaimed.

"Me, too," Rose said.

"I guess so," Mark said, following the enthusiastic group, wishing he could relax on this adventure.

Peter's bow and arrows were strung on his back. Meriwether had provided armor for Rose and Mark, but they didn't have any weapons yet. Luke wasn't sure how Mark's drawing magic would help them, but he saw Mark strap his satchel across his back and carry his drawing pad and pencil in his hand. Luke ignored the urge to take out his yo-yo and ease the tension in the quiet forest. He had to stay alert. Keeping his knees bent, so that he would be able to move in any direction, he imagined himself sparring with the older teens in his karate class. He remembered what Instructor Adam said about keeping his guard up so he wouldn't get hit. He drew his sword and kept it in front of him. Very little light came through the trees, so Peter took out his iPhone and turned on the light. He wanted to be ready in case any of those hairy trollics showed up again.

Rose stopped to pick up a red rock she thought was pretty and put it in her pocket. She heard a sound behind her. Luke had just walked past as she peered over her shoulder. "Ahhh!" she yelled when a hairy animal on two legs ran toward her swinging a stick. She couldn't see his eyes or nose, just a big mouth with jagged teeth.

Peter ran back toward her. "I'm coming!"

Luke attacked other creatures that scurried out from the forest cover.

When the hairy beast got close enough, Rose shut her eyes and kicked. "Kick and cover, kick and cover," she repeated over and over again. The beast ran away scared, but Rose kept kicking.

"Rose!" Peter yelled. "It's gone!"

"Huh?" Rose stopped and opened her eyes. "Did I hit it?"

"About a hundred times! Didn't you feel it?"

"No, I was too scared."

"Well, it's gone now."

That's what they thought until they heard many angry trollics getting closer.

"Run!" Luke called.

They ran in the direction of the lake, jumping over fallen trees, dodging roots, and holes.

"I see light!" Luke yelled. They ran out of the forest, but the trollics kept coming.

"We have to find a way to block them," Luke said.

Mark drew at a frantic pace. The forest appeared on his sketchpad, alive in pencil. He drew each of them with the lake in the background. Mark's hand was a blur. No one disturbed him. Next, he built a wall made of stone that reached as high as the trees and stretched across the width of the forest. When he looked up, sure enough a wall separated them from the trollics.

Luke slapped Mark on the back. "Nice work, bud."

Mark smiled just a bit, thankful it had worked.

"It looks deep," Rose said, peering into Crystal Lake. "I can't see the bottom."

"Meriwether wouldn't have asked you to do this if she thought you couldn't," Luke said. He peered at his crystal. It was clear, so they had a lot of time.

"What if something happens down there?" she asked.

"I'll tie a rope around both of us. If you're in trouble, just yank, and I'll pull you out."

"We don't have any rope."

"Yes, we do," said Mark.

He had drawn a thick, corded rope, and Peter held it. They tied the rope around Rose's waist and then around Luke's. Luke was the tallest and broadest, so they thought he would be strongest if Rose had to be pulled out of the water fast. Plus, even though no one had mentioned it yet, Luke seemed even stronger and healthier in this world. No one knew what that meant and avoiding the question seemed to be the answer right now. They removed their sneakers and socks and stepped into the water. It was deep, green, and the bottom felt squishy.

"It's cold," Rose complained, her lips turning blue. "You

know I don't like swimming in cold water!"

"Rose, it's about 70 degrees out. You'll be fine," Mark said.

"Hurry. He's very upset," Peter said. He tried to hum a lullaby, but the egg wanted nothing to do with it.

"All right." Rose checked the knot around her waist. It was secure. She looked back at her brother who nodded encouragement. "Well, here goes nothing!" She dove into the water. The rope followed her like a tail. Luke felt a tug and knew they were out of rope. He just hoped she had gone deep enough.

They waited. Peter looked at his watch and could see the egg, but not Rose. "One Mississippi, two Mississippi, three Mississippi." He began to worry at one minute.

"She's taking a long time," Mark said, as he doodled with nervous tension.

Luke treaded deeper into the murky water and shifted his face closer to the surface. "Even she can't hold her breath that long," Luke replied. He tugged on the rope to see if she would respond. Nothing. "I'm pulling her out."

Before he could, Luke was yanked underwater. He sputtered for air and tried to regain his footing. "Help me pull the rope!"

Mark dropped his sketchpad and ran in after Peter who held onto Luke, dragging him back. Luke reeled the rope in. Rose's hands broke the dark surface grasping a pale blue and green speckled colored egg. She screamed, but they couldn't understand her.

"We got you!" Mark yelled and yanked the rope, determined to get his sister to safety.

"Snakes!"

"Get my sword, Peter!" Luke called.

Peter ran to where Luke had left it on the ground and

rushed to his brother with sword in hand. He couldn't do much more than that. He kept covering his ears, trying to calm the egg. It was upset and very cold. "Pass me the egg, Rose!" he yelled.

"Don't worry about the dumb egg, Peter!" she screamed as another snake wrapped around her arm.

Peter didn't even notice. "I need the egg now!"

Angry beyond words, Rose threw the egg high into the air, while squealing about the snake on her head. Peter ran back a few feet like he did in baseball and caught the egg without cracking it. Rose fell back into the water, but Luke was close enough to catch her. He tossed her behind him and sliced his sword through the water. Mark ripped any remaining snakes off his sister and pulled her to shore. The snakes hissed and receded back into their watery hideaway.

Rose marched up to Peter and yelled, "You care more about that egg than about me! I could have been killed!"

"Shhh!" Peter said, not looking at his friend. He held the egg in his palms and rubbed it while blowing on it at the same time. The egg's pale color slowly changed to a deeper and more vibrant bluish-green. "There now, you're safe and warm." He sang the song *'Twinkle, Twinkle Little Star.'* The egg settled. He slipped it in his pouch and kept the egg under his shirt where it would stay warm.

Not able to help herself, Rose smiled at how gentle Peter was with the egg. As rough as he was when he wrestled his brother and Mark, he loved babies. It didn't matter what they were—human, monkeys (he probably loved those the most), koalas, or baby dragon eggs. Peter was a mush when it came to anything baby-like.

Peter finally peered up at Rose to ask if she was all right, but gasped instead. "What happened to you?"

"What do you mean? I rescued the egg and got attacked by snakes!"

"Guys! Look at Rose's neck!" Peter grabbed her arm and spun her around to face them. Their eyes widened to saucers.

"What's wrong?" She touched her neck and screamed, "What is it?"

"You have gills, like in my drawing," Mark said, as if he was talking about the weather.

"That's how you were able to stay under for so long," Luke said. "You were breathing underwater!"

"Tell us what happened," Peter said, his attention completely on his friend, now that the egg was happy.

As upset as Rose was about her neck, she was excited about what it had been like to be underwater. "Well, I swam lower and lower, but I was nervous because I couldn't really see where I was going. Then I knew I wouldn't have much air left. I started to turn back, but as I did, the water became clearer. I could see all around me. You wouldn't think there could be amazing fish in such gross water, but there was. I became so involved in swimming with the fish that I forgot to breathe."

"How can you forget to breathe?" Peter wanted to know.

"I'm not sure. I didn't forget really, I just felt like I was breathing as if I was up here. Then I saw the egg and picked it up. I was fine until I started to swim back. All these horrible snakes coiled around my legs. I swam faster than most of them, but there were too many." Rose shivered.

"You're safe now, and you saved another egg," Mark said, and he wrapped a heavy blanket around her to stop the shivering.

Luke checked his crystal. "We need to leave. The crystal is turning gray, and we have to get home before it turns black."

They raced to the entrance of the forest and into the wall that had protected them earlier.

"How do we get around that?" Rose asked.

"Do you think the trollics are still on the other side?" Peter asked at the same time.

"Easy," Mark said to Rose's question. He took out his eraser and rubbed the wall in his book. The wall disappeared as he erased.

"Be ready," Luke said, but the trollics were gone.

The friends tried to stay along the same path. The sun was on the far side of the forest and cast long shadows upon them.

"Hey, Rose," Peter said and pointed to her neck.

She touched her neck. The gills were gone. "Thank goodness. That would be hard to explain to Mom."

Luke whistled for Shimmer as they reached the clearing. She spiraled above them and landed. They jumped on, and Shimmer propelled them into the sky. As they flew toward the castle, the sun blinked a red hazy farewell behind them.

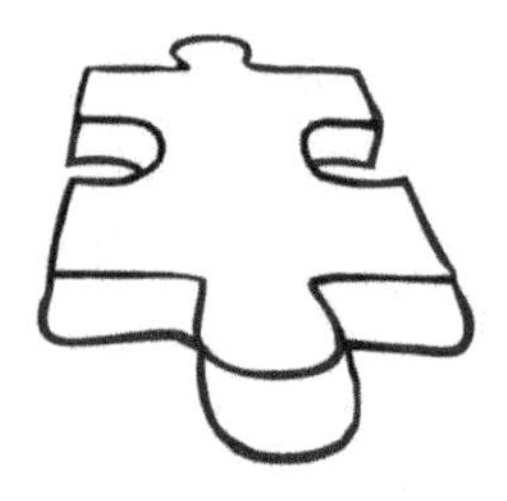

Chapter Five

Peter placed the egg next to its sibling and stepped back. This egg had turned an iridescent color and water oozed from it no matter how many times it was wiped.

"I found my powers," Rose told Meriwether.

Meriwether hugged Rose and said, "I am happy for you. Your patience will bring you many rewards."

"We're running out of time," Luke said. "We have to leave now."

Meriwether smiled at Luke. "You are stronger here." Luke nodded sheepishly. Everyone else was surprised that Meriwether had said what the others had been thinking. "I hope this means your wish is coming true. Thank you for keeping your friends safe. All of you have done well. Until next time."

The friends walked over to the puzzle and there was a picture of the turtle cave at their pool. They touched it and with a flash were gone. They fell onto the concrete floor with their legs and arms sprawled over one another in the tight space. Luke removed the puzzle piece, and it no longer shimmered with magic. Rose let out a sigh. Her brother patted her shoulder. She looked at him in surprise, and he just shrugged.

"Let's swim!" Peter said. They jumped into the warm pool water and swam as if chased by slimy snakes.

Rose and Peter were in their school gym during summer camp. Peter juggled his soccer ball from his knee to his foot, to his other foot, and back to his knee. Then with a flick, he kicked it in the air and watched it swoosh through the basketball net. Peter loved soccer and practiced any chance he could. Rose shot her basketball right through the hoop. Rose liked both basketball and swimming, but she only played recreational basketball right now while she was on the swim team.

When they stopped for a drink of water, Peter said, "I have a new lullaby for the eggs," and hummed a few notes.

Billy Bryce picked that time to lumber toward them and smacked Peter on the back of the head. He laughed. "Are you singing lullabies to your little girlfriend?" he taunted.

Peter's ears turned bright red. "She's not my girlfriend!"

"Oh, but you're singing baby songs to her!"

Peter didn't like being singled out by anyone. He felt the other kids staring at him. He wanted to find the anger like the Hulk, but only felt embarrassment.

"Ignore that big bully!" Rose said, pulling her best friend away.

Usually Billy would let it go, but not today when he had them all to himself. He was still mad about the town pool. He stepped in front of them, blocking their way. "Who are you calling a bully, fish face?"

Rose's hands flew to the sides of her neck, and Peter checked to see if her gills had somehow popped out. Her neck was normal. They both burst out laughing.

"What's so funny?" Billy bellowed, not liking how this

was playing out.

"Yeah, what's so funny?" Luke asked walking up behind Billy, as he performed a forward pass trick on his yo-yo.

Billy turned and glared at Luke, but his eyes widened with a hint of fear as the yo-yo swung inches from his face. Luke met Billy's stare with a lop-sided grin.

"Hey, Billy. Are you sharing a joke with my little brother and his friend? I'd love to hear it."

"No, uh, yeah, but I was just leaving." He shoved past Luke.

"See ya," Luke said.

"Thanks, Luke," Rose said.

Peter mumbled a less heartfelt thanks to his brother and sulked off to the cafeteria. He should have been happy that Luke was able to go to camp. Peter missed Luke's slumped shoulders and frown, as he massaged his arm where Billy bumped into him.

Rose sat down next to Peter and said, "You did great back there. You can't let Billy get to you."

Peter shrugged. "I wish I could say what I want like Luke does. He doesn't care what anyone thinks."

"It'll happen. Like Meriwether said to me, you have to be patient."

"I guess." Peter looked around to make sure no one could overhear them. "How are we supposed to get back to Shimmer and Meriwether?"

Rose picked at her peanut butter and jelly sandwich. "How about if you and Luke sleep over after karate tonight?"

Peter cheered up. Billy could tease him all he wanted, but Peter was the one on the amazing quest. "OK! I'll check with my mom, but I know she'll say yes."

That night was Peter and Rose's blue belt test. Rose's kicks were quick and exploded with power. Peter hit the heavy bag and imagined Billy's face. He always felt stronger and more confident when he wasn't the center of attention. He wished he could remember what he learned in class when he really needed it.

Rose went first for the self-defense part of the test. One by one her fellow classmates would attack her by grabbing her with one or two hands.

"Grab Art Two!" Instructor Adam yelled. A fellow student named Kim grabbed Rose's gi top with both hands. Rose stepped to her left and did an inside block with her right hand, then chopped toward Kim's neck and ended with a kick to her midsection. Kim grunted as Rose's kick hit its mark. No one wanted Rose's kicks to connect.

It was Peter's turn. An older student grabbed his gi and wouldn't let go no matter how hard Peter hit his arm.

With quiet assurance, Luke said, "You can do it, Peter."

"Peter, remember to 'kiyah' even when attacking. Be strong and believe in yourself," Instructor Adam said. "Grab Art Eight!"

Mark stepped forward and grabbed the right side of Peter's gi with his left hand. Luke was close by and said in a low voice, "Remember what you are fighting for."

From the look on Peter's face, Luke knew that his little brother was thinking of those eggs. Peter made a mean face and yelled. He yanked Mark's hand off with ease and stepped back into a horse stance as he knocked Mark off balance onto the ground.

Luke patted Peter on the back, and said, "Now I'm scared."

After another hour of kata and sparring, Rose and Peter stood at attention. Instructor Adam and the other teachers presented them with their new belts. The hardest part of the test was holding their belts out straight until everyone else received their own.

"That was great!" Rose said as she tied her belt around her waist.

"Yeah, but hard," Peter added. "I'm glad it's over."

Rose and Mark's mom brought all four of them to the house. Peter had packed the puzzle in the suitcase between his pajamas. The kids ran upstairs announcing they were going to build Legos. After he took his medicine, Luke joined them. They went into Mark's room and spread the building blocks all over the floor. Mark and Luke got involved in building a castle like the one Meriwether lived in, as well as different areas on the map. They had Vikings set up as the trollics. They were the Lego knights who would defeat them. Rose and Peter rolled out the puzzle. It had changed to display fancy tents set up around an open field.

"How does it do that?" Rose wanted to know.

"Must be magic," Peter said, shrugging.

They slid the puzzle under the bed for later.

When it was time to go to sleep, they hurried to brush their teeth, put on their pajamas, but had their clothes ready for when the parents went to sleep. Peter slept on the floor in Rose's room, while Luke was in Mark's room. They all lay awake, quickly closing their eyes when Rose and Mark's mom peeked in on them. Finally, they heard her go to bed. Low sounds from the TV filtered over to them. Rose snuck out of bed and quietly opened her parents' door. Both were asleep with the TV still on.

She closed the door and whispered to Peter, "Come on." Peter went into Mark's room while Rose got dressed. After Rose changed, she snuck into her brother's room and closed his door. The puzzle was on the floor.

"Ready?" Luke asked.

They all nodded, barely able to contain their excitement. Luke placed the last piece. Within seconds, the puzzle came alive and Meriwether stepped out of a tent.

"It is so nice to see all of you again," she said. Her eyes were sad with dark circles under them.

Shimmer flew up into the air and landed on the Yankees ceiling fan above them. She hopped from blade to blade and then settled on Mark's bed.

"You don't look very happy," Rose said.

"I am not, Lady Rose."

"What happened?"

Meriwether smoothed the folds of her burgundy dress lined with black trim, and her body shook as she took a deep breath. "Lord Tam has called for a tournament."

"Wow, a tournament!" Peter started. "We always go to the Renaissance Festival, and they have jousting and live chess games."

"Shh, Peter. This is serious!" Luke said, feeling a headache form in the base of his skull. The medicine he had that day always caused it. He took a sip of the caffeinated soda that helped with the headaches.

"I am being serious," Peter retorted, as he stuck his tongue out at his brother, not caring at the moment that his mom had told him to be extra nice to his brother and keep an eye on him.

Mark glared at Peter as he had been told the same thing and asked, "What does this mean for the eggs we still need to find?"

"The tournament will include sword fighting, wrestling, apple throwing, and wheelbarrow racing. It is a combination of bravery, physical prowess, and accuracy."

"OK, but what does this have to do with Shimmer's eggs?" Luke repeated Mark's question.

Meriwether sobbed, all traces of the princess gone. "I am the prize. Lord Tam believes he can win since my kingdom has so few knights. And if he does win, then the search for the eggs will be over."

They gasped. "He doesn't have the right to tell you what to do or make you the prize! Why doesn't anyone stop him?" Rose asked in a rising voice with fists clenched.

"All right. Let's keep quiet so we don't wake Mom and Dad. When is this tournament?" Mark asked.

"Today," Meriwether said. "But it is no use. These warriors are experienced and have trained their whole lives to compete in every event. Everyone is afraid and will only come so it looks like there is competition."

"We have tricks up our own sleeves, don't we?" Luke asked peering at his team. They looked doubtful. Luke petted Shimmer's back and pretended to pull a quarter from her scales. He showed his most enthusiastic smile. "Well, don't we? I have been fencing for a long time and protected myself against those trollics. Mark, you have been on the wrestling team for two years and, combined with karate, your techniques have got to be better. Peter has been playing baseball since he was four and can hit any target. Rose is light and has a strong upper body from swimming. She can be the wheelbarrow and one of us will hold her legs. We can do this!"

Peter saw the desperation in his brother's eyes and noticed how frail his brother had become. Of course they would do whatever was needed to get his brother's wish granted. Did they really have a choice? A determined smile spread across his face. "You're right, Luke. We can't doubt ourselves. Not when so much is at stake."

Luke looked at Rose and Mark. "Well?"

Rose was excited, but Mark was still skeptical. "I don't want to let anyone down. Especially you."

"The only way you would let us down is by not trying," Luke said.

"Well, all right."

"Great, then let's go. We have a lot to do so we can continue searching for the eggs."

Meriwether wiped the tears from her eyes and smiled at her friends. "It gives me great joy to know each of you. I am honored by your determination. Thankfully I can be there with you, since Tam invited me, and he is the one who holds the curse. Now let us go. Touch the puzzle if you please."

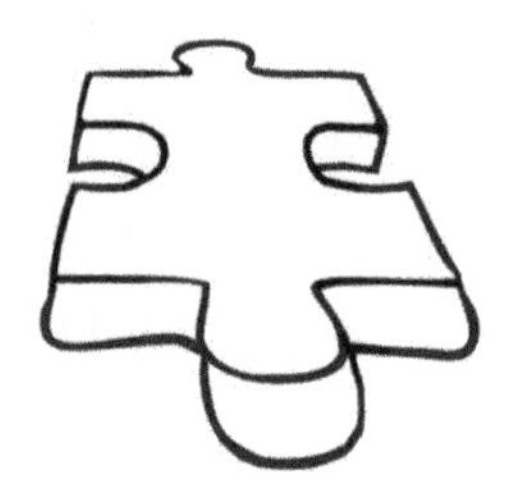

Chapter Six

They landed inside an elaborate tent. Squires were polishing armor and preparing swords for the tournament, and no one commented on four kids dressed in jeans and t-shirts appearing out of thin air.

Meriwether entered the tent smiling. "Deep in my heart, I hoped you would come, so I prepared."

Luke would participate in the first event. The squires helped him with his leather tunic and placed chain mail over his head. It was heavy, but Luke thought he would be able to handle it. His legs and forearms were covered with metal guards. He wore gloves soft enough to allow him a good grip on his sword, but also protected the back of his hands. Last was a silver helmet, topped with a large burgundy feather. It fit snug on his head like a ski helmet, but covered his cheekbones and mouth. Luke could see out the front well enough, but had a hard time seeing side to side. He had to turn his head to view what was next to him.

The others had changed into burgundy tunics and breeches, including Rose, since she would be walking on her hands. They didn't think anyone would want her to wear a dress doing that!

They wore vests embroidered with Meriwether's coat of arms—a dragon in mid-flight shooting flames from its mouth.

They walked out of the tent into what looked like a reality show for medieval times, except they were the participants. This was exactly how Luke envisioned it would feel like in the Renaissance Festival. He took in everything so he could give his uncle some ideas. Tam's castle loomed ominously beyond the arena and even the ever-present sunshine had slipped behind heavy clouds. The arena wasn't as big as Meriwether's, but a large square had been marked off for sword fighting and a roped circle for the wrestling match. The targets Peter would have to knock over stood at the opposite end. Surrounding all of this was an oval track that Luke figured was for the wheelbarrow race. To their left was a long line of bleachers that looked just as rickety as old wooden steps. They were filled with villagers, and Luke was surprised it hadn't collapsed. The air smelled ripe with horse dung, and Luke could see where the spectator's horses were lined up like they were starting a race. To their right, Tam and his rather large group of guards stood high on a platform that was covered in black cloth. The coiled gold symbol of a snake flapped in the wind on a flag. As they approached, the crowd cheered with the beat of a drum. When they arrived at the square, everyone's gaze shifted from the kids to the other end of the field. Luke wished he hadn't looked when he saw what was coming toward him.

"Oh my!" Rose exclaimed.

With every step this fighter took, the ground rumbled. With every wave of his arm, Luke felt a breeze. Each part of his body must have weighed more than a horse. When the giant paused in front of Luke, he realized that the man was really only as tall as his dad, but boy was he built wide. He was the size of the actor in the Terminator movie that Luke had been allowed to watch with his dad. Luke smiled and attempted to say hello, but the giant just growled.

"Mommy," Luke said as his legs shook.

"You'll be faster, Luke," Mark yelled from the side. "Remember to move and hit weak spots. It's not any different than fighting in karate class!"

Luke wanted to tell his friend that nothing they had ever done in karate came close to this reality. But he didn't, because he knew Mark was only trying to help him.

The horn sounded. Luke raised his sword and quickly rolled out of the way when the warrior swung his blade exactly where Luke's head had been. The rules were light contact, and the fighter who connected to any part of his opponent's body with his sword three times would be the winner. Not only would that strike have scored, it would have sliced Luke in two.

He needed to be faster and smarter. Luke took a deep breath and watched the man's shoulders. As soon as his shoulder moved, Luke lunged to the left. He whipped his sword to the right connecting with the warrior's middle. The giant roared. The audience stood in shocked silence. Rose, Mark, and Peter yelled wildly. Luke waved to them and felt the flat part of a sword hit his back. He fell hard and rolled out of the way as a sword sliced down at him. The crowd went mad, yelling for their brave warrior to finish him off. Luke didn't want to know what that meant.

Luke shifted around the field, trying to dodge the giant man's fierce blows. He moved close to his friends and yelled, "A little help here!"

Mark opened his satchel and took out a pencil and his drawing pad. "Think about punch attacks!" Mark yelled. He drew at a furious pace. When he finished, Luke's left arm was covered with Kevlar, like the woven material that police officers used to protect themselves from bullets. Luke felt the heavy weight on his left arm and saw the thick armor. The warrior thrust his sword at Luke. Luke stepped into a low fighting stance and blocked the warrior's arm with his left arm. The warrior winced, and Luke slammed his sword into his opponent's leg.

The large man roared in anger and swung his sword back and forth as he ran at Luke. Luke spun and raced around the fighting field. He knew it looked like he was running away, but this guy seriously wanted to hurt him. Luke didn't want any part of that sword hitting him. The warrior was big, so Luke hoped he could tire him out. He kept running.

As the warrior slowed down, Luke sidestepped to the left, swung around, and smacked his opponent's torso with the flat end of his sword. The horn sounded to end the battle. The man roared in defiance and rushed after Luke again. Luke ran toward his friends. Just as the angry warrior was about to lunge at Luke, he fell backward. There was nothing there, but the warrior was flat on his back. Luke looked over at Mark's sketchpad and saw a large square labeled 'invisible wall' where the man was. He laughed and hugged his friend.

"Thanks," he said.

"Sure," Mark said, erasing the wall and Luke's Kevlar. "No one said we couldn't use magic and, if this Tam guy is going to fight dirty, then we have to fight smarter."

Castle Dragonia was awarded the first round. Now it was time for the wrestling match. Mark placed his pencil and pad in his satchel. He handed it to Luke. "Don't let anything happen to this," he said.

"I won't. You can do this, Mark. Just believe in yourself."

"Right," Mark said.

Rose and Peter stood behind a fence so they didn't interfere with the ref. "You can do it, Mark!" Rose yelled.

"Yeah, do it for Meriwether!" Peter said.

Mark lifted his hand to acknowledge what his sister and Peter said. His blue eyes were solemn as he took in all the people and knew that this was bigger than an ordinary wrestling match. Mark felt the pressure to succeed. He was just a kid, what did they expect from him? *The best*, he thought, and that was all he could do.

A willowy young man approached. He was tall and lean, but Mark could see the rippling muscles coursing through his arms and legs. Mark was dressed in a one-piece singlet, which was skin tight and sleeveless. He was strong, but his body still hadn't developed a lot of muscle.

They stepped into the middle of a roped circle. Once again, the horn sounded. The two wrestlers began in standing positions and circled one another. Mark kept an eye on his opponent's arms and waited for him to attack. He tried to grab Mark's arms and pull him forward, but Mark kept turning his hands to the outside in circular motions. It kept his opponent from grabbing on. Then the young man grabbed Mark around the waist and swung him around. Mark fell to the ground and his opponent leaned over and grabbed Mark around the waist, so that Mark's head was in between the other wrestler's legs.

"Pop your head out!" Luke called. Luke had been to numerous wrestling matches and knew that Mark was in a bad position.

This guy is strong, Mark thought, *but I'm smarter.* Mark

shifted his head to the left, grabbed behind his opponent's knees, lifted him straight into the air, and slammed him to the ground in one motion.

"There you go, Mark! Get him on his back!" Rose yelled.

Mark's opponent flipped onto his stomach and managed to get to his feet earning one point for the escape. The horn sounded. Round one was over. Mark had one point, but his opponent had two. First wrestler to pin the other or reach five points would win the event.

Since his opponent had more points, Mark had to go down on his hands and knees with his butt on his heels to begin the next round. His opponent loomed over him, but Mark kept his focus. *He may be bigger than I am,* Mark said to himself, *but I'm fast. I have to know some moves he never learned.*

When the horn sounded, Mark immediately stood, pivoted to his right, reached back with his right hand, and grabbed his opponent's legs. Using this leverage he quickly yanked the opponent's legs out from under him, rotated on top of his back, and pushed him to the ground. Mark straddled across the back of the other wrestler and grabbed his arms trying to turn him over. They rolled out of the circle and a horn was blown. They regrouped. Mark tied the match at two points. The third and final period had Mark over his opponent with one hand wrapped around his opponent's waist and the other on his elbow. He started the round by chopping the other wrestler's arm at the elbow and pushing him forward at the same time. This forced him to fall forward on his belly in a flattened position. Mark worked so hard to get him on his back, but now his opponent had him partly on his back. Mark flipped him over his head and rolled him up on his shoulder, but then

Mark was under the wrestler again. It was never going to end! They were both on their hands and knees, struggling to get the other on his back.

"Mark looks exhausted," Peter whispered to Rose.

"He'll do it," Rose said, squeezing Peter's hand.

"Break him down!" Luke called, completely focused on his friend.

Mark popped up and circled his opponent. He shoved him back and then pulled forward, bringing the other wrestler to the ground. Then Mark grabbed an arm and flipped the wrestler onto his back. Mark pounced on him, wrapped an arm around his neck and another behind a knee. He knew that there were seconds remaining and wasn't sure if he had enough points to win. He tilted the wrestler back, so that his shoulders were touching the ground and held on. The referee had his cheek on the dirt waiting to see if both shoulders stayed down. He blew his horn and the match was over.

He won! Mark shot his arms up in the air and yelled, "Yeah!"

Luke ran out onto the field and lifted Mark up high. The crowd cheered, surprised and impressed by the strangers.

They hurried off the field so they could prepare for the apple-throwing contest.

Meriwether hugged them both and said, "Well done, Sir Luke and Sir Mark. You have proven that the desire to do good can beat even the biggest or strongest opponent."

Luke cast a glance where Tam now stood. Rage turned his face beet red, and he was whispering something to one of the guards. Luke hoped they would be able to get out of this place once the tournament was over.

Everyone followed Peter to the target stands. He stepped

forward to throw apples at the straw targets that looked like mini scarecrows. Ten were lined up on hay bales. There were five opponents including Peter. Every one of them was taller with longer arms. If they stretched far enough, it seemed like they could reach out and touch the scarecrows. Whoever hit the most targets won the match. Peter went first. He had a bucket full of apples. He lifted one and twisted it in his hand. It was true that he had been thinking about not playing baseball anymore, but he still had a strong arm and was naturally accurate. His uncle was always telling his dad that he should focus on baseball or basketball, because he had good hand/eye coordination, but Peter loved running around the field playing soccer. Besides he had good foot/eye coordination too, didn't he? He hoped whatever skills he had didn't fail him now.

Peter held the apple out toward his target and closed one eye. Then he cocked his hand back toward his ear and launched the apple at the first target. It went down. The crowd cheered. Peter smiled. The next one hit its mark and so on down the line. The last scarecrow looked smaller to Peter, but he knew that it had to be the same size. He took a deep breath and kept his eye on the target. The apple flew through the air and knocked the scarecrow over.

"Yes!" Peter yelled. He ran over to his brother who high-fived him and waited for the next match. Only one other opponent hit all the targets, so the rest were eliminated. As a tiebreaker, they had to see how many of the apples could be thrown through a hole. They were given ten apples once again.

Before they began, one of Tam's guards spoke to the ref in charge of the event. He nodded, even though the frown on his face showed his disapproval. He announced, "Lord Tam requests the opponents use their other hand for this round."

His opponent groaned. It had been a while, but Peter could throw with each hand. Peter studied his target. It was about as far as first to second base, so he knew he could reach it. He looked over at Luke.

"You got this!" Luke called to his brother and gave him the thumbs up sign. Peter kept his eyes on the hole and threw the first apple. It hit the edge, but went through. One after another, the apples made it through. Only one left. Peter shook his arm out, threw, and missed! His jaw dropped open.

"Oh no!" Rose cried covering her mouth with her hands.

"It's all right, Rose. We have to hope that this guy misses," Mark said wrapping his arm around his sister.

His opponent threw the first three straight through and missed the fourth.

"Yes," Peter whispered under his breath, hoping this would be over soon. He made the rest. The judges spoke together to see what to do about this evenly matched pair.

The hole was made bigger and one judge brought out a large ball of hay that was wrapped in twine. It was the size of a soccer ball. Peter smiled, but kept his head down. The judge explained that the challenger who could kick the ball through the hole would win.

"That t'ain't fair!" Peter's opponent yelled.

The judges ignored him and decided that he would go first. He held the ball and then placed it on the ground. He kicked the ball, but it went over the hole.

Now it was Peter's turn. He picked up the makeshift soccer ball and bounced it on his knee. He stared at the hole and then down at the soccer ball. He juggled it a few times and then placed it on the ground. The crowd was silent. Peter glanced over at Luke. His brother raised an eyebrow as if to ask, "What's up?" Peter thought about all the times Luke spoke up for him when he couldn't find his own voice. Now it was his turn. He could do something to save his brother. Peter remembered what his dad always told him before soccer tryouts. Play with confidence and never give up.

Peter stepped forward with his right foot and kicked the ball with his left. The ball rocketed straight through the hole. The crowd cheered and banged their feet on the wooden bleachers. The man who lost kicked the hay on the ground and stalked off.

"Luke, did you see that? Right through the hole!"

"That was great, Peter, really great."

Meriwether beamed at them. "You have all done so well and now we only have one more event. We need two of you to participate in the wheelbarrow race."

"I'm going to be the wheelbarrow, but I need someone to hold my legs," Rose said.

"I'm fast, but I don't think I can hold Rose for that long," Peter said.

They looked at Mark. "There's too much pressure. I don't want everyone to fail because of me," he said.

"I'll do it," volunteered Luke. But he looked at Mark and said, "Although I know you could do it." He removed his armor and joined Rose.

"You must circle the field twice," Meriwether said. "But beware. Others have been known to knock their opponents off balance. If you fall more than three times, then you are out of the race."

Rose pulled her blond hair back into a ponytail and stretched her arms over her head.

"Ready, Rose?" Luke asked, watching the other racers.

She shook her arms out like she did before a swim meet and nodded. "I'm ready."

Rose knelt on the ground next to the other opponents. She kicked her legs up and Luke held them tight, not wanting to drop his friend. Rose straightened her arms and tightened her stomach to keep her body from bending. The horn sounded and they were off. Rose's arms were a blur, and Luke had a hard time keeping up with her speed. As they turned to sprint around a pole, one of the other racers shoved into Luke. He dropped Rose's legs. Her arms crumpled under her. She fell into the hay and dirt, cutting her hands.

"That wasn't very nice!" Rose yelled at the others as they hurried away.

"Don't worry about it, Rose. Let's get back into position," Luke said.

They easily caught up with the back of the pack, but Luke was getting tired and Rose's arms shook. "My hands are burning, Luke!"

Luke struggled, but refused to let her legs go. "I know, Rose. Dig deep and keep going. We're almost there!" Sweat stung his eyes, and he took gulping breaths to fill his lungs.

Mark watched from the side. "Looks like they may need some help."

He drew in his sketchbook and suddenly Rose's palms turned into horses' hooves, but her fingers covered them! She laughed and took off like a thoroughbred. Luke stretched his legs as far as they would go to keep up with her. He could have used some hind legs himself! They trotted around the other racers and took the last turn at lightning speed. One racer tried to trip Luke, but he jumped and kept going. They could see the finish line.

"Duck!" Luke did. A heavy stick touched his hair as he and Rose flew past the finish line. Mark immediately erased the drawing and Rose's hands returned back to normal.

"You did it!" Peter yelled. They all hugged each other and Meriwether was swept into their embrace.

The horn sounded ending the tournament. This amazing team faced Lord Tam on his makeshift throne. He scowled down at the group. His face was pockmarked with eyes as hard as black rocks. He sneered at Meriwether like he was really the winner. When he addressed the audience, he revealed an egg in a red velvet basket!

Meriwether couldn't help the outrage she felt and yelled, "That egg belongs to Castle Dragonia! You have no right to hold it!"

Lord Tam returned the egg to the basket and said, "It is no matter since you and all the eggs will be mine anyway. It would seem that you and your children have managed to win every event. However, according to my rules, all contestants must be male."

Meriwether's mouth opened to object.

"You're not happy that a girl beat you!" Rose yelled.

"Yeah, and that egg belongs to Shimmer, not you!" Peter said.

Meriwether placed a hand on each of their shoulders to calm them down. They stopped and crossed their arms. "The rules were not made known to us beforehand, and therefore I ask that you let the win stand. As you know I have no desire to be wedded to you. You must return that egg and tell me what you did with my parents and Copper."

Lord Tam raised a thick black eyebrow and his face reddened at the fact that she would speak to him so rudely in front of his people. "Oh do I? It seems to me that I owe you nothing anymore. The ruling stands. The egg and you stay with me. Those annoying children will be removed."

Rose gasped as guards moved toward Meriwether. Peter had been whispering to Mark as Lord Tam announced his decision. A soccer ball appeared by his foot. He flicked it in the air and, turning his foot toward Tam, struck hard. The ball hit the bottom of the basket and a charcoal gray egg flew into the air.

A screech sounded above them, and flames flew over Lord Tam's head. He and those surrounding him fell to the ground. Shimmer scooped her precious egg out of the air and landed in the middle of the arena.

"Hurry, everyone!" Meriwether said.

The kids rushed toward Shimmer. Peter took the egg from Shimmer's mouth and tucked it in his shirt, humming the melody to *'Baa Baa Black Sheep.'*

"Attack them!" Lord Tam yelled. Two guards grabbed Rose. She screamed, bucking her head and kicking her legs. All three boys connected with their own kicks and punches and freed Rose. They scurried onto Shimmer's back as she spit fire at their enemy. She launched into the air and quickly flew back to Castle Dragonia with everyone hanging on.

Meriwether took the egg from Peter and placed it in the basket. Peter sat down next to the basket and sang *'We are the Champions'* to them.

"That was close," Luke said.

"Yes, and now Lord Tam knows we have at least one egg. He will launch an attack very soon. He is more terrible than I ever knew."

"Princess, we have to get back now," Luke said. His crystal

was the darkest they had seen it yet.

"Of course, be on your way. I will hide the eggs in case they should attack. Until next time, my friends."

Mark's room appeared in the puzzle, right down to his Yankees posters and bedspread. "How do they do that?" he wondered. The friends touched it and spiraled back into Mark's room. They fell with a thud.

"We'll talk tomorrow," Mark said. Rose and Peter snuck back into her room, but sleep took a long time to come for any of them.

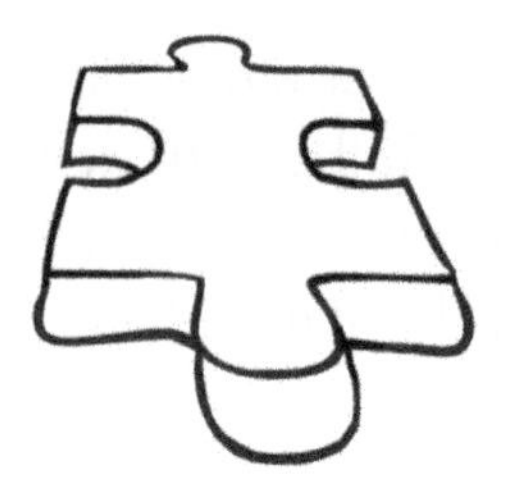

Chapter Seven

On Sunday, the two families left for their annual trip to the beach in Cape Cod. The kids were excited, because there would be two or three chances for them to visit Meriwether. Time was growing short, and they were still missing two dragon eggs.

They raced down to the beach on their first day. Rose and Peter immediately jumped into the water, even though it was cold. They raced to the six-person raft their dads had anchored in the water and launched themselves over the edge.

Luke and Mark had brought all sorts of tools and buckets to build a sand castle. Every year there was a contest for all the families who stayed at the Cape Cod Seashore cottages. Mark had drawn a rough draft of Meriwether's castle and together they began to reenact it with sand. By lunchtime they had the cliff built with tiny Monopoly houses stuck along a path to the castle. Two girls about their age stopped to admire their work.

"Can we help?" they asked.

Mark glanced at Luke who was pale and sweaty. Luke's

bald head was covered by a safari type hat which also protected his sensitive neck. Mark said, "Sure, but first could you help us bring that tent over the castle? It's pretty hot out, and I don't want to burn."

The girls were more than happy to help and after Mark handed out water bottles to everyone, they started on the castle. The girls were from Canada and enjoyed running back and forth to the water to get more buckets of wet sand. Luke and Mark soon lost themselves in the intricacies of the castle, making sure the balcony was the right length and the three towers had lines along their walls. The arches in the arena were the most difficult to erect, but once they did, the castle looked like the world that they had become a part of.

Rose and Peter had gone from the float to paddle boarding, but were now eating a snack and reading books from their summer reading list. They made kissy faces at Mark and Luke and, if the sand castle didn't look so amazing, they would have attacked it with sand bombs.

Luke's parents came down to the tent, and his mother bugged him to go in the cottage to get some rest. He knew he had been in the sun too long, but they were almost finished. Plus he didn't want the girls to know he was sick. This was the first time Luke had hung out with girls who looked at him as more than a friend. He didn't want to appear weak, but he was feeling a bit nauseous. Mark took some photos of the castle just in case the tide wiped it out. They made a huge moat in front of it, but you never knew at the Cape.

The girls had to go back to their beach, but promised to return the next day.

As they put the last touches on the castle, Luke turned to Mark and asked, "What did you say?"

His friend's eyes were a little glassy, so Mark asked, "You

all right, Luke?"

Luke shook his head, but heard the voice again. This time he said, "It's Shimmer." His eyes widened, and it wasn't his illness that made him pale. "We need to get back to the cottage."

Mark helped Luke stand and all four parents jumped up to assist. Peter and Rose were getting ready to go back into the water, when Mark said, "We're going back to the cottage to chill out. Why don't you two come with us?"

"I can take him back," Luke's mom said.

"You relax, Mrs. C. We got this." At Mark's raised eyebrows, both Peter and Rose said that they needed to get out of the sun for a while, too. They promised to text their parents if Luke needed anything.

Luke stumbled a bit going up the steep stairs, but Mark and Peter each held onto an arm and Rose carried their stuff.

They quickly changed and made sure Luke was comfortable on the bed. Peter and Rose pulled the puzzle out from under it. Almost as soon as they had arrived, they set up the puzzle, so Luke would only have to put the last piece in.

Luke drank some water. He popped a piece of his Double Bubble gum and was blowing bubbles, so everyone knew he was feeling a bit better.

"I heard Shimmer," Luke said as he grabbed his yo-yo and flicked his wrist so that it returned to his palm. Using his hands helped to soothe the worried sensations Shimmer was sending him.

"No way!" Peter said.

"Yes way, and something's wrong. We have to get there now!"

"Well then, put the piece in!" Rose said.

Luke did. Only Meriwether came.

"Hurry," she said.

The kids touched the puzzle and plummeted into times gone by. They landed in the inner courtyard. Meriwether and Shimmer waited.

"What's wrong, Meriwether?" Mark asked.

"There has been word that Lord Tam plans to invade my lands to take the eggs. He claims they are his by right of conquest. He will stop at nothing to get these eggs, which are due to hatch any day now."

"What is left on your map, Mark?" Luke asked.

"The rock mountain and the cave," Mark replied.

"Which one do you feel, Sir Peter?" Meriwether asked.

"It's very high. He's being kept warm and cozy," Peter said and sang, "Hush little baby, don't say a word."

"He must be on top of the mountain then," Luke said. "If Shimmer flies us up there, we can grab the egg and come right back."

Peter checked his watch and finally a small blip on the screen showed that the egg was at a high altitude.

"Shimmer cannot fly up there. Mount Isdor is on Lord Tam's land. They will shoot her down as soon as they see her. You must climb it yourself."

"Everything's a challenge," Luke muttered, but he would never stop trying.

Shimmer was able to bring them close to the mountain base where they would continue on foot. Luke peered up the mountain, but couldn't see the top.

"I'd rather be skiing down that mountain than climbing up," Rose moaned.

"The egg's in trouble," Peter said. "It's squealing. I think the other eggs are hatching. If the momma bird finds out that it isn't her egg, she might throw it out of her nest."

"Then let's hurry," Rose said.

Meriwether hadn't exaggerated when she said it was a mountain made of rock. There were craggy spots to put their hands and feet, like a rock wall.

"How are we going to get up there?" Mark asked.

Luke had an idea. For the last two summers, he had been to an outdoor survival camp. They learned how to use carabiners and rope to keep each other safe while climbing anything.

"Mark, can you draw some climbing rope, metal stakes, four carabiners, and straps to go around our waists, and a crossbow?"

Mark didn't question Luke's request. He just drew. The carabiners dropped onto the ground next to the straps, the rope untwined off the page, and the crossbow popped into the air.

Luke showed them how to put on the straps and passed the crossbow to Peter.

"What do you want me to do with that? I don't know how to use it," Peter asked.

Luke demonstrated and explained at the same time. "First, you pull the bow back and notch the arrow. Then you raise it against your shoulder, aim with one eye, take a deep breath, and when you breathe out, hold it, and shoot."

"How do you know this stuff?" Rose asked.

"From my comic books," Luke said. "Peter, you have the best accuracy of all of us, and you already know how to shoot a regular bow and arrow. Aim toward the top of the mountain. The rope is attached to this arrow. It'll help us climb the rock."

"But what if I miss?"

"You don't have time to miss, Peter. Think of your egg," Rose said.

Peter nodded and studied the mountain. He couldn't see the top, but he aimed the crossbow and let it fly. The rope soared up through the sky like it had its own wings. They heard a twamp and thunk sound. Luke pulled on the rope. It held.

"Nice job, little bro. Let me go first. Rose is next, then Peter. Mark, I'll need you to bring up the rear."

They began the climb with steady determination. The rocks hurt their hands, and it was difficult to fit their feet in the small spaces. At specific intervals, Luke placed a metal stake in the rocks and hooked another carabiner on it. Peter tried to soothe the egg as much as he could, but he had to concentrate on each movement to avoid falling down to the bottom.

As they climbed higher, Mark heard a swooshing sound. He yelled, "Something's coming!"

A large wing appeared out of nowhere heading toward Mark's face. Mark lost his balance and fell back against the rocks. Luckily their stakes held.

Rose strained to see her brother. "Are you all right?" she yelled.

"Yeah, but I don't think this bird is happy about our visit!"

Luke reached the top with relative ease and pulled the others toward him. Rose scurried over the edge and kissed the ground.

Luke leaned over to get Peter. In front of him a gigantic eagle beat its wings in anger. Luke estimated its wingspan at about six feet.

"Nice birdie," Luke cooed.

The eagle made a shrieking sound and flew at Luke. He

fell onto his butt.

"Help me up, Luke!" Peter yelled from below, struggling to pull himself over.

Luke army crawled to the edge. "Give me your hand!"

Peter reached up, and Luke grabbed hold. The eagle came swooping down, its sharp talons pointing toward Luke.

"Get away!" Rose yelled. She grabbed a stone and threw it at the angry bird. She hated to hurt it, but her friends needed help. The eagle screeched and shot up into the sky.

Luke heaved Peter over the edge and together they grabbed Mark and pulled him up.

They hurried over to the nest. "Here's the egg," Luke said.

"Look how cute these eaglets are!" Rose said.

The eaglets were brown and white with fluffy feathers and blindly reached their beaks toward the sky crying for food. The nest was about as wide as Luke was tall and, at his last check up, Luke had finally reached five feet. The egg they needed to rescue was much bigger than Shimmer's other eggs. It was in the middle of the nest that was sunk so low one of them would have to climb into the nest to retrieve it. Peter scuttled over the edge, scooped up the dragon egg, and heard it coo.

"He's happy now, but boy is he big," Peter said.

"Yeah, but that momma eagle is mad," Luke added.

The four friends glanced up just as the eagle launched toward them. She lunged her razor sharp talons and spiky beak at the kids to make them lunch for her babies.

Mark scratched away at his pad, while Peter hopped out of the nest and settled the egg in his secure pouch. They backed away from the nest toward the other side of the narrow mountain.

Suddenly, a huge raft like the one they had at the beach

appeared in front of them.

"Sorry, it's all I could think to draw," Mark said.

"What about water?" Luke asked.

"Oh yeah." Mark drew like mad as water sprayed over the edge of the mountain.

"Let's go!" Luke said.

The others hopped in, and Luke gave the raft a shove to the edge. He jumped in as it spiraled downward, just as the eagle's talons scraped his back.

"Hold on to the handles!" yelled Luke when he saw Rose and Peter bouncing into one another.

If they had wings, they would have flown. They reached the bottom of the mountain in record time. Mark erased their equipment, and they sprinted as Luke whistled wildly for Shimmer. The eagle continued to chase them deciding that they were worth the effort. Shimmer's large, shining form appeared over the canopy of trees. She flew straight toward the eagle, which twisted up toward the sky and flew back the way it had come.

"Thanks, Shimmer!" Rose called as they hurried onto her back.

As Shimmer began to take off, the kids heard yelling behind them. Mark was at the end, so he turned.

"We have another problem! I think Lord Tam's men are chasing us!"

"Hurry, Shimmer," Luke mind-spoke.

As Shimmer shot up into the sky, one of the arrows Meriwether had warned them about pierced her underbelly. She bellowed and the right side of her body dropped. The kids screamed, but Shimmer righted herself and flew on, crashing onto the castle balcony. The kids jumped off and yelled for Meriwether.

She quickly assessed the situation. "Help me lift her wing. We must get this arrow out immediately."

The kids heaved and lifted the enormous wing. The shaft was about four feet long. Meriwether took hold of the arrow and pulled it out as quickly as she could. Shimmer growled in pain.

"It's all right," Rose cried, but she shivered when she saw how much blood was on the large arrow point. She was so upset, Rose didn't even comment on the fact that Shimmer's blood flowed like liquid gold.

Meriwether cleaned out the wound and wrapped it as best she could. Shimmer crawled into the main area and collapsed by the fire.

Peter took out the egg and placed it in the basket. The other eggs sighed in happiness.

"This is getting too dangerous. That was one of Lord Tam's poisoned arrows. He will stop at nothing to get these eggs. One of you might have been killed!" Meriwether said.

"We have a job to finish," Luke said. "We only have one egg left. We can't stop now."

"According to my drawings, there is only the cave left," Mark said.

Meriwether looked at Luke, then the others. They had all grown from their experiences here, and she had never known braver or smarter knights. "You are right, of course. Knights do not stop until their quest is done. Hurry home. We must hope that this egg is saved before it hatches, but it will be your hardest challenge yet."

"Why?" Mark asked.

"The cave is also on Lord Tam's land, and many who have traveled inside have never returned. And now you must hurry. How much time do you have, Sir Luke?"

Luke pulled out his crystal and realized that it was almost black. "Oh my gosh, we have to leave now!"

They were at the puzzle, which pictured their room at the cottage. They all reached to touch it.

"My crystal!" Luke exclaimed as it fell to the floor, the strap broken in two. He bent down to pick it up, but everyone had already touched the puzzle. Luke felt a wave of dizziness come over him as he touched it. He disappeared a few seconds later.

Mark, Peter, and Rose appeared next to the bed. "Where's Luke?" Mark asked spinning around.

"Oh no, oh no!" Rose screeched. "He was left back there!"

Peter's face paled as he called out for his brother. No matter how much they argued and fought, he loved his brother and didn't want him to be stuck in a different world. Before Peter could panic, he said, "Let's look outside."

They ran around the cottage and searched behind the other cottages along the main path. "It's OK, Peter. We'll find him," Rose said.

"Find who?" Rose's dad asked walking up from the beach. Peter's dad followed close behind.

"Where's Luke?" Peter's dad asked.

Peter broke down and sobbed, "We don't know. He didn't come back with us."

His dad's face creased with worry. "What do you mean didn't come back? I thought he came up here to rest. Did you guys walk down the road?"

They all looked at one another. They couldn't say where they had been, because they couldn't get back and their fathers would never believe them. So they did what they could to buy some time hoping Luke was just a little delayed.

"Yes," Rose said in her best sorry voice.

"Why would you do that when Luke was feeling sick?" Rose's father asked.

"We, uh, were playing scavenger hunt. We only meant to go a bit down the road," Mark said. "Plus Luke was feeling better."

His dad looked intently at Mark. He felt his face redden, because his dad had to know he was lying.

"Go to the beach and tell your mothers what's going on. We'll go look for him. Which way did he go?"

The kids all pointed in different directions. "Let's split up," Peter's dad said.

Luke landed hard like he fell out of the sky. Standing, he called out to his friends and brother. He felt dizzy, and when he looked at his bare arms, he noticed his rash was back. None of this looked right. "Peter! Rose! Mark! Where are you guys?"

Since they had been inside the cottage, Luke didn't have shoes or a hat on his head. He could feel his sensitive skin burning. His head hurt, and he was extremely tired. He walked a little farther toward where he thought the cottage would be.

Luke noticed the ice cream place called Why Wait Until Sundae and realized where he was. Unfortunately, it was a mile away. Luke was scared and instinctively, he grabbed for his sword and felt vulnerable when it wasn't there. He was no longer in Shimmer's world fighting trollics and evil knights. He was in his world. It should have made him feel better, but when a wave of nausea overtook him, Luke squatted down on the sidewalk. He reached into his pocket remembering his phone, but the battery was dead.

Out of the corner of his eye, Luke noticed an older man in a convertible slow down. The man called out. "Are you all right?"

Luke knew that he shouldn't talk to strangers, but he had kind eyes like his grandpa. Images of the evil Lord Tam flashed through his mind, but he really had no idea how long he had been gone. He said, "I'm not feeling well, and I'm about a mile from the cottage where I'm staying."

When Luke told the man the address, he responded, "Oh yes. I know where that is. I'm heading that way and could drive you there."

Luke hesitated. "No, that's all right, but if you wouldn't mind stopping and letting my parents know where I am, I would appreciate it. I'm sure they are worried by now."

The man smiled and said, "You're a smart boy. I will certainly do that for you."

"Thanks, my dad's name is Lou. He's tall and has short black hair." The man nodded and drove away.

About ten minutes later, Luke recognized his dad's red Toyota 4 Runner. Luke waved his arms frantically. His dad hopped out of the truck and helped him stand. Luke hugged his father.

"How did you get so far away from the cottage?" his dad asked, not happy about the situation.

"Something caught my eye. I followed it without watching where I was going," Luke said. He felt bad about lying. His parents always said that lying was the worst thing you could do, because it broke a person's trust in you. But he thought that once Shimmer's eggs were safe, they would write an adventure story for their parents. Otherwise they may not let them go back.

"Well, I'm not happy that you went off on your own

without telling us, but I am glad you didn't get in a car with a stranger. I know you want to be on your own more and that it's been hard for you, but your mom and I worry more because of your illness."

"I know. Thanks for coming for me," Luke said feeling even worse. "I think I need to cool down and rest." He hated he had made his parents worry. Just when he was becoming a teenager it felt like he was being treated like a little kid because of their fears. It wasn't fair and that gave Luke even more reason to finish his quest. One more egg, and everything would be fine. He could go to school like a healthy kid.

Once Luke got back to the cottage and listened to three other parents berate him then cluck over him with concern, Luke excused himself and walked up to the bedroom.

"What happened?" Rose asked, jumping up from the bed they were all huddled on.

Peter hugged his brother. "We thought we would never see you again!"

Luke raised an eyebrow at his brother's show of affection, but hugged him back.

"Welcome back, Luke," Mark said nodding.

Luke plopped down on the bottom bunk bed and let out a big sigh of relief. "Thanks. I dropped my crystal and released my hand from the puzzle. All of you disappeared before I did. I got dropped off a mile from here. It was really weird."

"It bothers me that you might have been stuck there," Mark said. "What would we have done if you couldn't come back?"

Luke could see that his friends and especially his brother

were shaken by his absence. It made him realize how much they meant to one another. "One of you would take the piece out of the puzzle, wait two days, and come back for me. We'll always be there for one another no matter what happens."

Something shifted among the friends and siblings. Their bond was built through family and friendship, but now it was forged by their loyalty toward one another and their fight for something bigger than themselves. Their success not only affected Luke's health, but the future of an entire village and family of dragons.

"And we need to be there for Shimmer and her eggs. We only have until next Friday before the eggs hatch," Rose said.

"Yeah, and our parents aren't going to let us out of their sight for a while, so we won't be able to go again while we are here," Luke said. "We'll have to figure out something for next week."

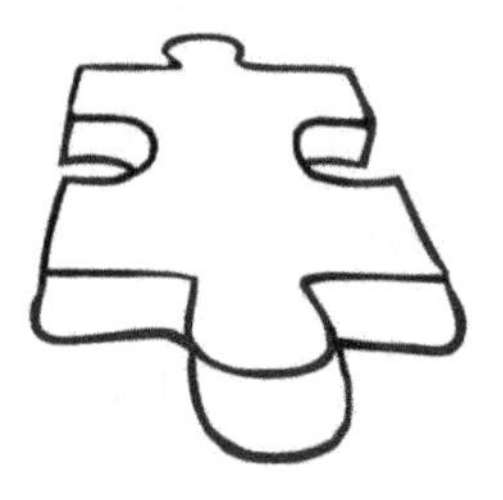

Chapter Eight

Their next chance was at Rose's swim practice at the YMCA. At the appointed time, a water-drenched Rose met them at the door of the family locker room.

"I found an empty changing room we can lock," Rose said.

There weren't too many people around and once the aisle was clear, they all scrambled to fit in the cramped changing room.

"Watch my toe, Peter!" Luke whispered in annoyance.

"Well get your elbow out of my ribs!" Peter yelled.

"Shhh!" Rose exclaimed. "People are going to hear us."

The boys settled down and unrolled the puzzle. It barely fit on the floor. Rose and Peter stood on the bench while Mark and Luke kept their feet next to the wall, so they didn't step on the puzzle. Something was odd about it. It didn't have that golden glow or gray wall behind Meriwether.

When Luke put the last piece in, Meriwether emerged, but Shimmer did not.

Fear flooded the children. "Where's Shimmer?" Luke asked.

Meriwether's eyes were rimmed with dark shadows, and her face was very pale. "Alas, Shimmer is not well. The arrow was truly poisoned. She does not have a great deal of strength. Come, I do not want to leave her for long."

"Wait a minute," Rose said. "I might have something that will help her." She squeezed out of the changing room and ran to her locker. She came back in and locked the door. "Let's go."

They touched the puzzle and ended up by a wall in the great room. Shimmer lay quietly by the fire with her eggs. Her scales had lost their luster, and she didn't open her eyes when Luke mind-spoke to her.

Rose knelt down next to Shimmer, removing the ointment from her bag. "This is triple antibiotic ointment that I use when I have scrapes. I thought this would help her."

"Rose," Mark said quietly. "She has a very large wound. You don't have enough to cover the infection."

Rose yelled at her brother, "Well, then draw some more! And while you're at it, draw a needle with antibiotics to give her."

"I don't know what type of medicine she would use! I could hurt her!"

"Not if you do it out of love. It'll work, Mark. I know it."

Peter stood next to Rose. "She's right, Mark. We need Shimmer to teach these baby dragons how to survive."

Mark looked at his sister, Peter, and then at Luke who nodded to him. "Oh, all right. I'll try my best."

Luke said, "That's all you can do."

Mark drew with the precision of a surgeon. He didn't want to accidentally give Shimmer something that could harm her. A large tube of ointment appeared, which the other three slathered on the infected area. Then a rather large needle appeared. Rose's face went white.

"I . . . I don't think I can stick Shimmer with that," Rose said.

"What is it?" Meriwether asked approaching them. She had been watching them work diligently.

"It's called a needle and has medicine in it that we think will help Shimmer," Luke said. "But we are all a little nervous to give it to her."

"If it can help, then I will do it," Meriwether said and pushed her sleeves up her thin arms. "How does it work?"

Luke said, "You poke her skin with this sharp end and then press this flat part down." Luke pointed to the plastic plunger on the syringe. "You'll be able to see when all the medicine is gone by looking on the side of the tube."

"Very well," Meriwether said and held her hand out for the needle.

All the children gathered around Shimmer and held her.

Luke mind-spoke to Shimmer, *"This might hurt a little, girl, but it will make you better."* Shimmer groaned, and so he said, "I think she's ready."

Without hesitation, Meriwether injected the needle in Shimmer's side and pressed the top until the medicine was gone. Shimmer flinched slightly, but otherwise remained still.

"There," she said. "Let us hope it works. Thank you once again. All of you have done so much."

"That last egg wants its momma," Peter said.

"Very well." A worried Meriwether beckoned them over to a thick oak table covered by a map. "This is Lord Tam's cave. A few years back we were able to sneak in and look around. It was rumored that Lord Tam was stealing our grain supply and storing it in the caves for his use."

"Was he?" Rose asked.

"He was stealing grain and more. He is a horrid man who only thinks of himself!" Meriwether said.

"Meriwether," Luke asked. "Where do you think the egg is hidden?"

Meriwether wiped a tear from her eye. "If he has found the egg, then I do believe that it would be hidden here." She pointed to a spot deep inside the cave. "There is a secret room where Lord Tam keeps his treasure. It is close to impossible to get in there undetected."

"That's just great," Mark said. "How are we supposed to get in and out of there without anyone seeing us?"

Luke scrunched his face in concentration and then threw up his arms with excitement. "I know! You can draw us invisible capes that we can wear. It'll be like in *Harry Potter* except we can each have our own so we can travel quicker."

"But how am I going to draw something that is invisible?" Mark asked.

Rose piped in. "You did it when the giant was attacking Luke. Just draw a cloak and name its properties, meaning that it can be invisible when you put it on. Oh, and make a small sack that we can carry it in."

"Good idea, Rose!" Peter said.

"Thank you, Peter."

"You are welcome." He turned to Mark. "Did you draw it yet?"

Mark blew the hair off his forehead. "No, I can't concentrate. Leave me alone for a bit."

They left Mark to finish his drawing and took turns petting Shimmer. She managed to open her eyes for a moment and then went back to sleep.

Luke quietly walked over to Meriwether who looked

so much older and drained. Luke's energy soared in this place, and he wished he could share it with his friend. "Meriwether?" She looked up at him and straightened as if remembering her position of authority. Luke put his hand on her shoulder, so that she leaned back and relaxed again. "How are we going to get to the cave if Shimmer can't fly us there?"

Meriwether tapped her cheek and replied, "I have been thinking on that, Sir Luke. Can you ride a horse?"

Luke's eyes opened wide. "Uh, no and I don't think I want to be on one of them. Are there any other options?"

"How about dirt bikes?" Peter asked. He had sneaked behind them to listen.

"Peter, we don't have . . . ," Luke started and stopped when Peter pointed to Mark.

"We have Mark, remember? He can draw us anything we need, and we need dirt bikes. You and I can drive Mark and Rose."

"But what about people seeing or hearing us? Won't they think we are witches or something and try to kill us?" Rose asked.

Peter replied, "We can make them electric so they will be quieter."

Luke pulled out a quarter from his pocket and twirled it around his fingers. It almost felt too easy. All the skills they had in their real world were working here in this time from the past. But was it bad to bring back all this modern technology? Maybe if they erased whatever they brought it wouldn't matter. Besides hadn't they already changed history by being here?

All these thoughts threatened to give Luke a headache, so he thought about what he could control. He didn't worry about riding the dirt bikes. Peter had learned to ride when he was four and had been racing for the past two years. Luke enjoyed riding on the trails and going over the large bumps on the track that his uncle had built on his farm. Peter tended to be more of a daredevil, going over jumps trying to get some air. He thought his tires flew off the ground, but he really only managed to lift the wheel slightly. It was all right, since he had fun. Both brothers had driven with passengers, so it really shouldn't be a problem. He couldn't help worrying about everyone's safety. After all, wasn't he in charge of protecting them? And weren't they all there to help save him? They were helping each other and building new friendships. His mom had said that it was always harder to accept help than give it, but both were equally important. It made him smile that he had such amazing people in his life.

"I'm done," Mark said. They all gazed at him as he held up four small satchels. In each was an invisibility cloak.

"That's so cool!" Rose said grabbing hers. "We had better test them." Rose pulled hers out. It was the color of lilacs. "Ooh, pretty color." She wrapped it around her neck, and everything below her neck disappeared.

"Ha! Rose, only your head is showing," Peter laughed so hard he fell over. Rose pulled up her hood and was gone.

"Rose?" he asked and then said, "Ouch," when she stepped on his stomach. "That's not fair!" Peter said, standing. "Give me my cloak, Mark, and we can have an interesting game of hide and seek."

"We do not have time for any games. You must go," Meriwether warned.

Peter and Rose looked chastised and, after everyone tested their cloaks and placed them in a bag attached to their armor, the kids went outside. They took the long trek down the hill to the valley where vast fields of grain and vegetables grew. Just inside the tree line, Mark proceeded to draw two dirt bikes that were big enough to be comfortable for two people, but not too much for Peter and Luke to handle.

"Now draw two sets of pegs, here and here," Luke pointed to where the riders' feet would rest, as well as the passengers'.

"Make sure we have brakes," Peter called out.

Rose sat on a rock and stared out at the water. Meriwether knelt down next to her. Gently placing her hand on Rose's shoulder, she asked, "What bothers you, Rose?"

Rose turned to the beautiful princess, tears welling in her eyes. Peter moved over to them and was shocked to see that Rose was about to cry. Rose never cried—not even when she played basketball and got knocked over by a bigger player. She was the toughest girl he knew. He waited for her answer.

"I have a bad feeling about this last egg," she said.

"How so?" Meriwether asked.

"I . . . I don't think it will come back."

Meriwether gave her a squeeze. "We can only do what we can and leave the rest for whatever may be."

"But there is so much at stake. How will it affect our wishes?"

All three of them looked over at Luke who had started one dirt bike and hopped off to start the other. He looked like a healthy 11-year-old boy getting ready to have fun with his friends. His skin was clear, and his cheeks were rosy. His brown hair curled tight around his head, and his smile was extra bright. They would have never known he was sick.

"You can only control what is in front of you. Sometimes you need to have faith to see you through the rest," Meriwether said and stood. "Come, it is time to go."

Both Rose and Peter obeyed, but sighed because their biggest question still wasn't answered.

It would have looked odd to someone watching them leave, since they were wearing medieval armor and dirt bike helmets. They didn't care. Rose rode on the back with Peter, and Mark rode with Luke. They waved to Meriwether and took the wide path along the forest.

When they came upon a fork in the road, Rose looked at the map Meriwether had provided for them and said, "Take the road going to the left."

"Are you sure, Rose? I thought she said we had to travel closer to the line of trees," Luke argued.

"The map points that way. I feel it strongly."

"All right."

The road became bumpy with large rocks in the way. The boys proceeded very slowly, not wanting to fall over and hurt anyone. The water was no longer visible and protruding walls of rocks jutted out on either side of them. Some small trees and vegetation broke through. The sky was dreary with thick gray clouds hovering over them. They could smell rain in the air and hoped to get to the cave soon.

"There it is!" Peter yelled and picked up speed to get to the entrance. The opening was large enough to pull their bikes in.

"We didn't think about having an invisible blanket to cover the bikes, did we?" Rose asked.

"I did," Mark said and, as he spread the blanket he had already drawn, the bikes disappeared.

"Great! Now as long as no one walks into them, we'll be fine."

"Hey," Mark said shrugging his shoulders. "I can only

do so much."

They donned their own cloaks and, after giggling about their bodiless heads, disappeared under their hoods.

The four friends continued giggling as they each made sounds. Luke pretended he was a ghost while Peter attempted to burp. Rose's sneakers squeaked, and Mark whistled nervously.

Away from the opening, the cave became dimmer, damper, and more mysterious. They paired up next to one another so they wouldn't get separated. Peter and Rose were in front and stopped abruptly causing Luke and Mark to bump into them.

"Be careful!" Rose hissed.

"Why did you stop?" Luke asked and then didn't need an answer as he peered past them. The cave floor simply ended and dropped into complete darkness.

Rose shoved her way back past the boys. "I'm not going down there."

It was never spoken aloud, but everyone knew that Rose feared the dark more than anything. She always had her disco bulb nightlight on when she went to bed and, if she ever got up at night, every light went on before she took a step into the next room.

"What do we do now?" Peter asked.

"Feel for the egg, Peter. Hum to it and check your watch. Where do you think it's located?" Luke asked.

Peter thought of a fun song he had learned in chorus. Humming *'Yankee Doodle Dandy,'* Peter tapped his foot on the dirt ground.

"Oh man!" Peter exclaimed looking down at the beeping light on his GPS. He hunched his shoulders.

Everyone knew that the location of the egg was through

the vast darkness. They all peered with fearful eyes over the edge. Luke was the first to act. He clicked on his phone's flashlight and shone the light down. There was nothing except more darkness.

"At least we know we are alone," Luke said. "We just need more light."

Mark removed his sketchpad and drew large floodlights like the ones his dad had bought to light up the ice rink they had in their backyard during the winter. Mark's dad was an avid hockey player, and he and friends played a game called broomball on the ice. Basically, they hit a ball around with brooms, but it was fun.

As Mark drew the floodlights, he thought about how they would get down to wherever the darkness led. They were pressed for time so climbing down a ladder would be slow and possibly dangerous. The blackness dissolved as four bright lights appeared around the cave.

"Nice job, Mark!" Luke said.

They looked over and could see that the bottom stretched out into total blackness. They hadn't expected much more, but it made them nervous to have to climb down into the unknown.

An emergency slide appeared. It was wide and the sides were high enough so that they could go down two at a time and not fly off the edges.

Peter nodded in glee.

"Let's do it," Rose said.

They packed their cloaks away. Rose and Peter linked arms and pushed off the top. They found it hard not to scream on the way down, but they both managed and flew off the end of the slide. They rolled and bumped into each other. Then Peter jumped up and scanned the area. Luke and Mark were on their way down. Their siblings ran to the sides, so they wouldn't get taken out like bowling pins.

Mark quickly erased the slide and lights, and Luke peered around with his flashlight. There were four tunnels. Checking his watch, Peter said, "They're this way."

Rose hesitated and said, "I don't think so. I have a bad feeling about this place."

Just before Peter walked down the tunnel, his watch beeped uncontrollably.

"Shut that thing. Someone is going to hear us," Luke said.

Peter turned his watch off and shut his eyes, humming to the egg. "I think it's this one." He moved in front of the second tunnel and again he heard sounds. When he really focused, he said he heard eggs from every tunnel.

"How can that be? Meriwether said there was only one egg missing," Rose said in frustration. She wanted to get the egg back to make Shimmer happy.

"Maybe Lord Tam has stolen other eggs," Mark suggested.

Everyone turned to Luke to wait for his response. He was deep in thought and didn't say anything for a while.

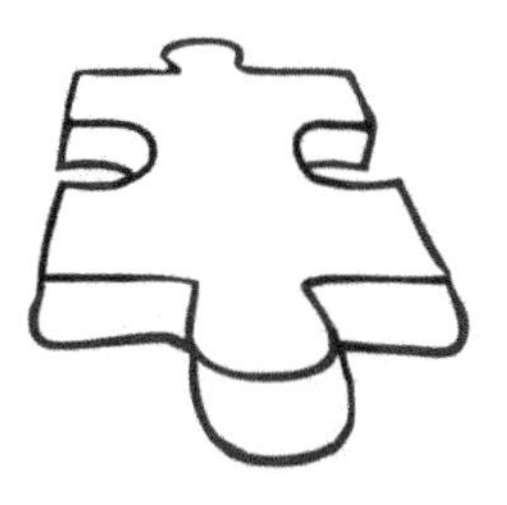

Chapter Nine

After a few more moments, Luke gazed at them. Luke felt older than his age and wasn't happy about it. He wanted to be carefree and fight with his brother all day. If he wasn't in charge here, he was sick in bed at home. It wasn't fun having all this responsibility resting on his shoulders. But it did and, as he saw his friends and brother counting on him, he couldn't let them down.

"I think it's a trap," he said softly.

"A trap?" Rose repeated, as she became very aware of her surroundings and backed up against a wall.

"Well, it makes sense. We have overcome every monster or obstacle Lord Tam has sent against us. He wants these eggs, and we have shown him up four times already. I think he's dealing with us himself this time."

"OK," Mark said taking it all in. "Then what do we do to protect ourselves? We can't leave the egg. It'll be evil if it stays with Lord Tam."

"Let's separate. We can each go down a different tunnel," Peter suggested.

"We can't separate, Peter! What are you thinking?" Luke spoke, his tone harsh.

"Why can't we? Just because you don't want to!" Peter responded.

"It's . . . ," Luke started to say dumb, but then saw his brother's face. His brother had also matured during this whole ordeal. There was a lot riding on finding these eggs, not only for them, but also for Shimmer and Dragonia. Everyone was fighting, and they were wasting precious time. Plus, Peter was emotionally attached to these eggs and wanted to do what was best for the babies. Luke knew it would be too dangerous to separate, but it wasn't necessary to put down his brother. He rubbed his eyes. Yes, he sure did miss the days when his biggest challenge was giving his brother a wedgie. He began again. "It's a great idea, Peter, but too dangerous. We need to stick together, find the egg as one group, and then leave together. We can't be in different places if we run out of time."

Luke waited for his furious outburst. "Makes sense," Peter said shrugging.

Luke almost passed out from shock. "All right, little bro. Which tunnel feels right to you?"

Rose, who had been unusually quiet during the brothers' argument said, "I think it's the one all the way to the right."

"Let's listen to Rose," said Peter.

Rose had been right the last few times, and her mom always said she had good instincts. Donning their cloaks again, they wound their way into the tunnel as Luke led with his flashlight partially covered.

When they finally came to two paths, they headed left. They were just starting to complain when the tunnel opened.

Peter stopped, listened, and then hummed. "I think we're on the right track. The egg is humming back."

They continued, renewed with hope that they would

rescue Shimmer's last egg. It was crucial to get all the eggs, since the dragon bonded to whomever it first saw when it hatched.

Peter had hoped he would bond with one of the dragons, but then he would have to leave it in Meriwether's land, and the poor dragon would be left without a friend. They continued more carefully, aware that this could be a trap for them. Luke withdrew his sword just as Peter notched an arrow in his bow.

Rose would kick anything that came close, and Mark had his sketchpad ready to draw their escape. As they rounded a corner, they could see a pale light illuminating the darkness. Luke shut off his light. Then the sound of chanting reached them. They stopped just before the sound became louder. Luke tried to peer around the corner to see what was happening, but was afraid they would see his face. Peter wiggled between Luke's legs with his cloak on and watched.

Then he shuffled back and whispered frantically. "It's a wizard! He's chanting some kind of spell."

Rose shook. "I think we should get out of here."

Just then the wizard turned and yelled, "Seize them!"

Guards jumped out and grabbed Peter as he tried to shift back under his invisible cape. Peter broke the grab with a block and kicked the guard in the knee. "Run!" he yelled.

Luke threw off his cape and jumped into the fight. There was no way anyone would get away with grabbing his little brother. Someone very large wrapped his arms around Luke's chest and squeezed. Luke felt the breath wheezing out of his lungs, as he was lifted off the floor. When he tried to hit the guy with the back of his head, he connected with his chest. That wasn't going to work. Luke remembered

Instructor Adam's lessons, so he let his body go slack. The guard loosened his grip, which gave Luke enough room to lift his arms and elbow the guy in the gut. Then Luke grabbed an arm and flipped the guard onto the ground.

When he became aware of his surroundings, he realized that his brother, Mark, and Rose were being held by sword point. How had this happened? Luke failed them all!

They were shoved against a pole onto the dirt floor and had their hands tied behind their backs. They faced each other, so Luke could see that no one was hurt. The guards left them figuring they weren't going anywhere.

"What do we do now? Your crystal is getting darker, Luke!" Rose cried, tears streaming down her dirty face. Most would have thought they were tears because she was scared, but it was more that she was madder than ever and her emotions always came out that way.

Luke looked around. He said, "Thank goodness they didn't take your bag, Mark."

Mark nodded. "If I could get untied, I could draw something to save us."

Peter said, "Try and call Shimmer, Luke. Maybe she'll hear you."

"That's a great idea." Luke shut his eyes and mind-spoke to Shimmer, *"We are stuck in the cave. Captured by Tam. Very bad. Need help!"*

After about 15 minutes, they really started to worry. Luke had his Swiss Army knife, but it was in his pocket. Rose had been very quiet and when she opened her eyes, she said, "I hear someone coming."

The guards untied them from the poles, but their hands were kept tied behind them. They were led into a big open area.

"It's Lord Tam! He's got the egg on some kind of stand!" Peter exclaimed.

The same wizard was on a stage saying something over the egg. The room grew dark. They had traveled toward the end of the cave, but could see the sun trying to shine through the rock.

When they approached, Tam sneered at them, "Brave, but stupid." His voice sounded deep and raspy.

Lord Tam was more than twice their size and was probably double all their weights combined. His dark hair was mangled and wild around his head. His eyes were as black as the cave had been and bore holes into the kids' eyes, making them want to look away. Peter shifted closer to his brother. When Lord Tam smiled they were met with gross cavity-filled teeth.

"Oohh," Rose said, not able to help herself. What would her mother say about teeth like that!

Lord Tam stepped closer. "So you thought to steal all the eggs for yourself."

"Those are Shimmer's eggs," Rose shot back.

He ignored her and continued, "I would agree that for such small creatures, you have done well. But it is over. This egg will hatch with me, and I will steal the others."

"What do you want with the eggs, anyway?" Peter asked.

"They will be my army. With them, I will take over all the lands around me, and Meriwether will be forced to marry me."

"No one would marry you with those teeth. Plus, you're mean!" Rose yelled.

"Quiet, Rose," Mark said.

"We want the egg," Luke demanded.

Lord Tam put his finger on his chin, considering and

then laughed. “No.”

Suddenly, Peter gasped as if he was in pain.

“What’s wrong, Peter?” Rose asked

“The egg. It’s buzzing really loud. It hurts. Make it stop.”

The egg in Tam’s hand began to tremble.

Luke and Mark had been whispering. Mark quickly removed Luke’s Swiss Army knife from his pocket, while the guards were distracted. He cut Luke’s hands free. Luke quickly did the same for Mark and then Rose and Peter.

“The egg is hatching. You are too late! Kill them!” he yelled to his trollics.

They grunted and ran forward. Luke grabbed a sword and met the puny creatures head on and swung at them like they were part of a video game. They disappeared into dust when he sliced through them. He was glad, because he didn’t want to see real blood.

Rose screamed and kicked anything that came her way. Peter ran toward Lord Tam, but then jumped up on a rock and threw smaller rocks at the trollics. They only got angrier. One trollic managing to dodge Peter’s rock smashed right into him. Peter fell off the edge and hit the side of his face on the ground. He didn’t move.

“Peter!” Luke yelled trying to get to his brother.

Not able to draw, Mark released a loud yell and began to punch, kick, and flip the monstrous creatures. He worked his way toward his sister to protect her, although from the size of the dust pile growing around her, she didn’t needed it.

An agonizing screech erupted in the cave, stopping everyone in their tracks. Lord Tam stared at the cracking egg in his hand.

Luke reached Peter, who sat up dazed. “We’re too late,” Peter cried.

At the same moment, the dragon's beak chipped away the last bit of shell that blocked its exit. Luke heard Shimmer cry. She was the one who had screamed. Her egg was lost, and she felt the separation.

The dragon lifted its head and peered at Lord Tam who smiled wickedly and then laughed insanely.

All four kids stood in stilled shock as the dragon's eyes glowed and shot a laser-like light into Lord Tam's eyes. But the surprise didn't stop there. As it shook off its shell and flapped open its small wings, the kids saw that it was the golden dragon.

Lord Tam lifted his eyes to the kids. They were no longer dark, but golden like his dragon. His dragon; no longer Shimmer's. And they were all going to be toast if they didn't get out of there fast.

"Shimmer, we have to leave now," Luke begged, but Shimmer's mind was too clouded with grief. Trollics banded together for one final attack.

Lord Tam whispered, "Attack," into the dragon's ear, and it appeared ready to listen. No humming on Peter's part made a difference.

Mark drew frantically, but he didn't know what would protect them from an evil dragon. As they stood together, sure that they would end their lives as pre-teens, the cave walls shuddered. Small rocks broke free and then larger ones crumbled down. The light disappeared, but not for long.

Luke had just enough time to yell for everyone to get out of the way before the ceiling caved in. They ran to the edges and, when the dust and rocks settled, Shimmer stood there. Her scales were still pale, but some of her color had returned. They swarmed onto her back. Shimmer radiated anger and blew trails of hot smoke toward Lord Tam. He held up the golden dragon, which hissed at the intrusion.

"You are of me, Golden Dragon," Shimmer growled to her egg and for a moment their gazes met. Something passed between mother and dragon. The dragon faltered at Lord Tam's command to attack the children, and it was all the time Shimmer needed to fly away. Luke stroked Shimmer's scales as they flew up into the sky, knowing that had probably been the hardest thing any mother ever had to do—letting your child go. He shivered when he thought of his parents losing him or his brother.

With battered hearts and bodies, the kids rushed to Meriwether. She gathered them into her arms. They were filled with grief and regret at their failure.

Meriwether pointed to the nest filled with four eggs. "You did not fail, and it is not over yet. That dragon has a connection to Shimmer and good and evil will war within until we can get it back."

"But how?" Rose cried. "Lord Tam bonded with it. We have nothing else!" Tears of sadness flooded down her cheeks, and her big blue eyes were rimmed with red blotches.

The noise that Peter had heard earlier echoed in his head. "Not again!" he said. This time the pain level brought him to his knees.

Meriwether took in Luke's healthy color and knew that there was more to this quest than their wish and saving Shimmer's eggs. Seeing how close these young warriors were to the eggs, she made a decision. "It is time. Come, brave warriors. There is more that you can do." Meriwether placed an egg in each of their hands.

They sat in front of the fire, weary and sad, but hope literally lay in their hands. They just didn't know it yet.

The eggs were calmer being held. Peter focused on his round egg as it vibrated. The baby dragon pecked at the shell, trying to make its way into the world. Peter couldn't think of a song to sing to the little guy. His mind was too excited wondering what the dragon would be like. To soothe the egg and himself, he rocked back and forth and hummed to the rhythm like his mom did with him as a baby. With wide eyes, Peter saw the first crack appear. A white eye tooth stuck out and then a round pale nose. The dragon clawed its way out to him.

"You can do it, little buddy," Peter encouraged.

A large chunk fell off the top and the dragon popped its round head out and peered into Peter's eyes. The flash of light caught Peter before he could look away. Then he couldn't. The legend of dragons floated through his mind. Their history and abilities became a part of his memory as well as what Peter would need to teach it. Likewise, Peter's whole childhood, all his memories, problems, hopes and fears flashed into the dragon's mind—and they were bonded, loyal to one another forever.

Peter felt a strong pull of love for the little guy in his hands who was busy kicking away the shell and flapping his wings to spread them out. The dragon was a pale blue with a black circle around one eye, and as round as Peter was when he was a baby. It crawled up Peter's arms and licked his cheek, which tickled Peter. He laughed, and then the dragon tucked itself in by Peter's neck and fell asleep.

"He's so round, but his eye makes him look like a pirate. I'm going to name him Patch," Peter said. He looked over at everyone else, and they stared in shock at him and the dragon that hung out on his shoulder.

Rose jumped when she realized it was her turn. Her

sparkly egg had already cracked and, as a piece of shell fell off, water dripped out.

"Oh! I think it went to the bathroom!" Rose said, disappointed that her dragon would do that.

"It smells salty, like sea water," Luke offered.

Rose leaned over, sniffed, and realized he was right. Then the egg split in two, and the dragon shook its body. More water than could have possibly been in that egg splashed over Rose.

"You're a watery dragon!" she laughed.

The sea-green scales shimmered like waves on the ocean. The dragon lifted her slippery head and looked into Rose's eyes with its own aquamarine ones. In Rose's mind, she was launched into the sea and rode with hundreds of dragons, seahorses and dolphins. The dragon roared happily when it saw how much Rose loved the water, too. They would have great fun together.

Rose's connection was broken when she felt the dragon nipping at her arm. It jumped and nipped like it wanted to play.

"You are feisty, but beautiful," Rose said. "I will call you Sparkle."

Mark nervously held his gray egg. He didn't want to break it and hoped that the dragon would like him. His egg cracked at the bottom by his palm. It took a while before the first piece came away from the egg. A charcoal gray dragon army crawled its way out of the shell, its small arms reminding Mark of a T-Rex, his favorite dinosaur. It sniffed around and then hooked its huge gray eyes onto Mark's deep blue ones.

All Mark could think was that this dragon understood him, even more than Luke. This dragon would share his love of books and knowledge, and Mark already knew that it had greater intelligence than most modern day geniuses. A sense of calm came over Mark and, as he petted the dragon's head, something black came off on his finger. He rubbed it on his sketchpad and realized that it was charcoal.

"So you're an artist, eh? But you're also brave and strong. I think your name will be Boulder," Mark said.

Luke was in awe of his friends' dragons. He loved all types of dragons, so to have one was incredible. Luke held the largest egg. Its shell was rough and seemed thicker than the other eggs, but soon began to vibrate in his hands. Not waiting to use its eye tooth to make a small opening, the shell shattered into bits as the husky dragon shot its wings out. It puffed out its orange chest and extended its wings as if showing off its muscles. Luke laughed and the dragon's eyes pierced his own. Luke's world as he had always known it was gone. Replacing it was the power of this strong creature roaring its impatience. Luke didn't know what his dragon wanted to do, so he spoke through his mind, happy that it responded like Shimmer did.

This dragon was a bruiser with an attitude. Any dragon that could break through an egg with its wings deserved the name of Luke's favorite martial artist.

"I will name you Norris," Luke said.

Mark smiled his approval.

"Well," Meriwether said in a choked voice behind them.

They turned to face her with their dragons comfortably in place. Each dragon reflected an aspect of its owner's personality and their bond would grow as they learned more about one another.

"Let the babies be with their mother."

Shimmer mewed to her baby dragons. Chirping the

whole way, they waddled or hopped to their mother. Before each settled on her warm belly, Shimmer made eye contact with each of her babies and created her own special bond with them. They curled up together and as newborns would, ate, and fell asleep.

Peter, Rose, Mark, and Luke were still shocked by their experiences.

Luke broke the awestruck silence by holding up his crystal. "We have to leave."

"You do," Meriwether responded.

"What about our dragons?" Rose asked, excitement turning to sadness.

"They cannot travel with you. Shimmer will care for her young and, when they are ready, you will come back to train with them. They grow fast so it should be by the first crop season. Then they will be ready to do what we ask of them."

"Wait," Peter said, holding up his hand. He sang, "Somewhere over the rainbow, way up high."

"Do you sense an egg, Sir Peter?" Meriwether asked.

"I do. It's hatched, but doesn't feel like a dragon. Would I be able to sense another type of creature?"

"Oh no! We have to find it. What will happen?" Rose said.

"Shimmer only had five eggs. I do not know what this creature is or where it hails from. You have to go," Meriwether said.

"But we'll miss them," Peter said, wanting to pick up his chubby dragon and rock him.

"As they will miss you, but you are connected and will have a sense of what they do and how they feel. They will feel you too, so do not fret."

"We have finished the quest. How will we know if we can come back?" Luke asked.

"You will know if your wishes did not come true. I am not sure that this quest is over. I call it an urging, a sense that you have to find them again. And you will dream of them as they dream of you. They will tell you if you need to come. Trust that you will know."

The kids were disappointed, but hoped when they arrived home, Luke would be better.

"Now off you go," Meriwether said as gently as possible. She led them toward the table and the puzzle that would take them back home.

Mark stopped and asked, "How will you protect yourself against Lord Tam? He'll be coming for Shimmer's babies."

Fear flashed in Meriwether's eyes, but she stood brave. "Shimmer and I will do all that we can. Our first priority is to keep these dragons safe. Now that the dragons are born, I hope they will lead us to Copper and my parents. We have been afraid for a long time, but the four of you have helped us to be brave once again."

They ran and hugged Shimmer and then Meriwether. With one last look, they touched the puzzle that would take them all lifetimes away from a world they had grown to love and had brought them closer together.

As the children faded from Meriwether's world, she glanced out the window and saw Lord Tam's banner flying in the wind just across the border. The battle for the dragons had begun.

Chapter Ten

It was the Friday of Labor Day weekend. Only a few more days until school started, but it had been a week since their dragons had hatched. Luke had been in the hospital since their last trip, so they knew their wish had not been granted. The quest wasn't over. The kids texted images and thoughts that popped in their heads during the day or while deep in sleep. Luke was comforted by both Shimmer and Norris' voices, but they were like whispers in the wind.

Rose texted, *"I had a dream about Sparkle last night."*

"Yeah, so did Peter about Patch." Luke texted back. *"I haven't had any dreams, but I feel like something big is going to happen that will change our lives forever. I'm coming home tomorrow. We should get together."*

Peter texted separately to Rose, *"Why don't you come over early tomorrow, and we can put the puzzle back together. My mom found it and took it apart."*

"I'll be there," Rose replied.

By 9am, Rose and Peter searched both Luke and Peter's room. Then they rummaged through his game closet looking for the puzzle of Meriwether and Shimmer. They emptied the shelves filled with games like *Hungry Hungry Hippo, Clue, Uno, Chess,* and numerous other puzzles.

"Where is it?" Peter fell back on his butt and pounded his fists on the gray rug.

"Let's ask your mom," Rose suggested.

"Good idea." Peter texted his mom who was at the hospital with Luke.

Her reply sent a chill through his entire body.

Rose shook Peter's arm. "What did she say?"

Peter stared at his friend. "She gave it away."

Rose screamed, "Oh, no! What are we going to do? Without that puzzle we can't save Luke!"

Peter thought quickly and then pulled Rose's arm to follow him. "Hey, Dad!" he called while stepping into the garage. His dad was working on one of his vintage motorcycles and didn't look up. "Rose and I are going on a bike ride."

At his dad's grunt, they each took a bike, threw on helmets, and took off. They started the two-mile bike trek to the local Salvation Army store. It was beyond where they were allowed to ride, but nothing mattered except finding that puzzle. Luke's life literally depended on them getting it back. Peter wouldn't think about how much weaker Luke had become since they came home. He wasn't sure what it meant, but without the connection to their dragons and Meriwether, they were lost.

Locking their bikes, they entered the single room filled with clothes, household knickknacks, books, games, and furniture. Rose marched right up to the counter and asked a gray-haired lady, "Excuse me, where are the puzzles?"

The lady removed her silver eyeglasses and peered at Rose. "Well. Let me see."

Peter let out a low growl of frustration and Rose shushed

him.

The old lady shuffled to a far wall. "This is where our games and kids' activities are stored. Puzzles are on the shelf," she said pointing to a bookcase full of puzzle boxes. There were smaller boxes scattered in a basket.

"Thank you," Rose said.

Peter pulled each box out even though he could see the puzzle's picture on the side. He wasn't taking a chance and missing it.

"What will we do if it's not here?" Peter asked partly to himself.

"It's here, Peter. It has to be. Too many people need us to find it. Keep looking."

They searched through all the puzzles.

"It's not here," Peter said, flopping his arms to his sides. "Now what?"

A second bookcase had books haphazardly stored on it. "Let's look through this. The box could be in this mess," Rose said determined not to give up.

Peter sat on a bench while Rose searched in a pile of boxes. Peter stared at the shelf thinking it was over. He would never see Patch again. Meriwether would never find her parents, and she'd be forced to marry that gross guy, Lord Tam. Luke would . . . a glint of color caught his eye. It shimmered with sparkling blue highlights. Peter stood and stared at a box on the top of the bookshelf. He found a stool and reached to grab a puzzle. Jumping down, he stared at the top cover. Realizing he stopped, Rose asked, "What did you find?"

Peter couldn't find the words, so he passed the puzzle to her. For the first time in their friendship Rose was at a loss for words. It wasn't the picture of Meriwether and

Shimmer reading a book together, but of dragons. Their dragons. They were huge, but absolutely Boulder, Sparkle, Patch, and Norris as they flew over their castle.

"I think we were meant to find this puzzle," Peter finally said.

"I agree. Let's buy it and get back to your house. We need to put this together," Rose said.

Luke arrived home from the hospital with his mom and Mark. He was ashen, and his father easily picked him up to help him into the house. His father brought him downstairs and laid him on the plush couch. Luke looked around the room that had been updated to a pseudo man cave for his return home. Posters from their favorite video games were displayed next to a signed poster from the New York Giants Eli Manning, whom the boys had just met at training camp.

After his dad left, Luke stared at the puzzle of four dragons and asked, "Where is the other puzzle?"

Peter and Rose started in at the same time. "Puzzle's gone . . . ," Peter said.

"Rode to Salvation Army . . . ," Rose began.

Mark held up his hands. "Slow down. We can't understand you."

Rose took a deep breath, got the nod to explain from Peter, and shot off like a horse at the starting gate. "Your mom gave the puzzle away!"

"And some of our games!" Peter piped in.

"That's sad, Peter, but not important right now. Anyway. She gave it away. Peter and I rode our bikes to town. We went to Salvation Army to buy it back, but it wasn't there. This one was there instead."

Luke stopped her. "You rode by yourselves?"

The younger siblings nodded and beamed with pride.

"And Dad let you?" Luke asked.

They both at least had enough sense to look guilty. Luke pulled out two marbles from his pocket and twirled them in his hand, whether from worry about what could have happened or excitement about the puzzle, no one was sure. "OK, but next time let us know."

All of them worked for an hour on the 500-piece puzzle, each separating the colors of their personal dragon, feeling closer to them as their forms solidified. They were down to the last piece, and Peter automatically handed it to Luke. Luke stared at it and gave it back to Peter. "You and Rose found the puzzle. I think one of you should put the piece in."

"You do it, Peter," Rose said.

Peter shrugged and said, OK." Peter held up the last piece, looked at his friends and brother, and placed it to complete the picture of his dragon, Patch. The puzzle glowed, but the dragons didn't pop into their world.

"What should we do?" Rose asked.

"Let's touch the puzzle," Luke said.

They touched the puzzle and shafts of iridescent light surrounded them. They arrived in the training arena. Meriwether rushed toward them as Luke fell to the ground, fainting. Luke woke up on thick blankets in the main room next to the fire. He moved his fingers and lifted his arms. His rash and even the bruises from his IVs were gone. Gingerly, he sat up and stretched.

Shimmer growled in greeting, and Luke stood to pet her. *"Yes, I'm much better now."*

He saw his brother, friends, and Meriwether on the balcony watching something in the sky. He joined them. They all clamored to be next to him, touching him, and hugging him while expressing their deep concern.

"I'm fine now. I think the journey was a bit too much for me coming right from the hospital."

"Look, Luke," Rose said taking his hand and pointing toward the sky with her other hand.

Luke gasped as he saw four huge dragons spiraling through the air. "How did they grow so fast?"

Meriwether said, "Time travels much faster here. A month has gone by and they are full-grown. We were very fortunate as Tam and his terrible trollics tried to break down our castle walls and have terrorized our villagers." Meriwether visibly shuddered. "And last time he almost succeeded. Shimmer was forced to fight against her own dragon. If she hadn't, all your dragons would have been captured. I don't think Cíartan was physically hurt. However, the training that Tam has pushed him through will make it harder for Shimmer to get him to come back to her. His name means black dragon and the longer he is away from us, the darker his heart will become."

"What do you need us to do?" Mark asked.

"I need you to train with your dragons as soon as possible. The time has come to rid our lands of this enemy." As the dragons swooped passed the balcony toward the arena, Meriwether beckoned them to follow her. "Come. It is time to train."

As they left the room, Meriwether motioned for Luke to stay behind. She placed a warm hand to his cheek. His face was cool, eyes clear. "Are you well?"

"I am much better here. I'll be fine and can do my part," he said not wanting Meriwether to think he couldn't lead the quest.

"I would never doubt you." She dropped her hand resigned. "Know that you always have a place here."

Luke's eyebrows scrunched together in confusion. "I know I do, but I don't want my brother and friends to worry so much. Everything will work out."

Meriwether's eyes filled, but she forced a smile. "Go join your dragon. Norris has been waiting for you."

She didn't have to ask twice. Luke bounded off to join Norris. Shimmer growled, and Meriwether touched her dragon's iridescent scales. "I know. He will figure it out. I only hope that his brother and friends will accept it when the time comes."

Shimmer flew out off the balcony and met them below. Shimmer shifted to the side as Norris saw Luke. He reared up onto his hind legs, expanded his chest, and flexed his wings like he was displaying some ripped python.

"Nice," Luke grinned. He wore his favorite red sleeveless t-shirt displaying the words USA in the colors of the American flag. Mimicking his dragon, he flexed. Norris roared in approval and wrapped his wings around Luke.

Rose shifted impatiently for Sparkle to land and was soaked to the skin by what felt like a waterfall.

"What was that?" Rose asked. She spun around at the gurgling sound and couldn't help but smile at Sparkle as she lay in a puddle of her own making. "You're a bad ginormous dragon, Sparkle, but so cute! I can't be mad at you!" Rose jumped in the puddles and splashed her dragon.

Mark stood away from everyone holding onto his satchel. He saw what only could be described as a large gray rock a few feet away from him. Moving closer he whispered, "Hey big guy, did you miss me?"

Boulder lifted his head and his eyes, now a deeper shade of gray, gleamed at Mark. The pencil tip colored dragon opened his wing, and Mark settled next to him. "Do you want to see my drawings of you?" He took what he thought was a nod and opened his sketchbook.

Peter had watched his brother and friends greet their dragons. Patch was hiding behind Shimmer and appeared content there. Peter wanted to see him very badly, but didn't want to scare him. So he hummed the song *'Bingo'* and clapped his hands. Out of the corner of his eye, he could see two dark blue eyes observing him. The circle around his eye was thicker. Peter hopped around and added some extra beats to his song as he slapped his hands to his sides. Without warning Patch waddled out from behind his mother and cooed. Peter's eyes grew large, and he was filled with love for this adorable creature. He was still rotund with baby fat, and his blue scales glimmered like a pale summer sky. Patch stopped in front of Peter and held his wings wide open. Peter ran into them, and they fell to the ground in a big baby hug.

Luke was astonished at these dragon creatures. Who would have thought that one day he would find not only one, but six? Well seven, but he hadn't met Copper yet. He always knew they existed, and he couldn't wait to write a story about them to share with his mom. He saw tears stream down Meriwether's face.

"That was lovely," Meriwether said clapping her hands together.

"Can we ride them?" Rose wanted to know.

"They need to get used to you first and be fitted with saddles. For now, let us talk."

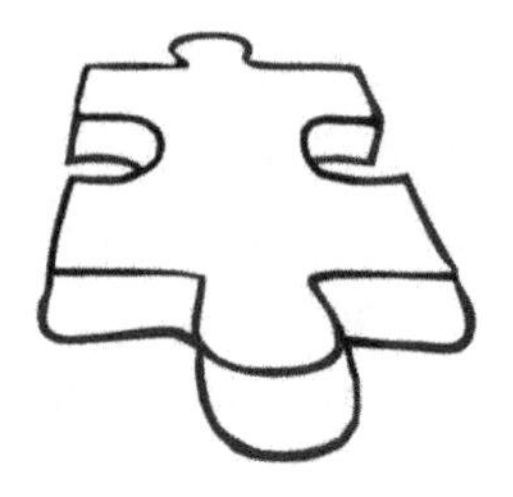

Chapter Eleven

"So you see, after the dragons hatched, Lord Tam waged war to gain my hand in marriage and take the dragons."

"Why doesn't anyone stand up to him?" Mark asked.

"Since both of my parents are missing and believed to be dead, no one wants to anger Tam. I should have the authority, but we do not have enough men to lead an attack. We only have enough to hold our castle. The hope is that now that you are here, you will be able to find my parents and save the golden dragon."

"Do you have any idea where your parents are?" Rose asked.

Meriwether rolled onto her knees and grabbed Rose's hands. "I think I do." Meriwether looked around her in suspicion, even though it was obvious they were all alone. "About a week ago, I received a message. All the knight could say was that an old man limping by his horse asked that he deliver an urgent note to me."

"What did the note say?" Peter asked.

Meriwether pulled out a piece of parchment and said, "It was a riddle:

'What goes up must come down, when a smile is a frown.

In the dark skies I flew to where the water and sky meet blue.

Back to the golden scales I have traveled, so that this tale may be unraveled.'"

"I have no idea what that means. It hurts my head!" Peter complained and covered his face.

Rose giggled, but Luke and Mark sat down and reread the riddle. Luke peered into his pocket Kaleidoscope as Mark reread the first line out loud. "What goes up must come down, when a smile is a frown."

"A rollercoaster," Luke guessed. "When you go upside down your smile is a frown."

"There aren't any rollercoasters here, Luke!" Peter said.

"Have you forgotten? Mark can draw one," he replied.

Rose sat down next to her brother. "Why would we need a rollercoaster?"

"I don't know, Rose," Mark said and wrote rollercoaster at the top of a blank page.

Rose read the next line. "In the dark skies I flew to where the water and sky meet blue."

"That sounds like the horizon over the water," Luke said and asked, "Where is the largest body of water? Do you know where it ends?"

Meriwether tapped her long finger against her chin and thought. She said, "I have never traveled beyond my land except to the Great Gathering that happens once a year. I have heard stories of ships traveling on water farther than the eyes can see. But that is beyond where I have been."

The kids knew this was true, but they didn't know if the land was formed the same here. "When is this gathering, and how many days does it take to get there?" Mark asked.

"Five days on horseback, and it is in a fortnight. I did

not plan to go this year because of all that has happened."

"Maybe some knights there can help you fight the evil guy," Peter said.

"It's possible. I had not thought of that."

"We could get there in one day if we rode our dragons," Luke said.

"Will they let us ride them?" Rose asked.

"They will, but they need to be comfortable with you, and they haven't flown for great distances. They are still young for that."

"Sounds like they need some intense training like the beginning of soccer season," Peter said.

"And swimming and basketball," Rose added.

"And wrestling. We could all help them," Mark said.

"That sounds great, but let's figure out this riddle. It's the key to the rest of this quest," Luke said.

Peter read out loud, "Back to the golden scales I have traveled, so that this tale may be unraveled."

Before anyone could respond, Meriwether jumped from her chair. "That is it! Why did I not know this before?"

"What is it?" Rose asked catching Meriwether's excitement.

"Let us go upstairs." The dragons followed making the room very cramped. She turned to the group. "This tale is shown on the ceiling above. Look." The kids lay on top of their dragons and viewed the visual tales of dragon lore. Meriwether began, "The dragons were not always able to have golden dragons. It was not until a male and his mate accidentally came upon a mountain that flowed with gold from its highest peak. Curious, the male flew too close and was splashed with the gold, which quickly turned the rest of his body the same color. Amazed, his mate touched the flowing gold with her talon and was also turned to gold.

"When they returned, some of the dragons feared this change. But others noticed that they flew higher, faster, and were stronger. When these two mated, one of their brood was also golden, while the others were regular dragons. Only the golden dragon possessed these special abilities.

"Wanting to be stronger and gain power, the leaders went to this mountain only to find that it no longer flowed with magical gold. The gold was solid. Several of the dragons became jealous and eventually these two dragons and their babies were forced to leave their home forever because they were different. They are Shimmer's ancestors. The golden dragon has continued through her lineage. Perhaps Copper and my parents have gone to this place, which is indeed far across the waters."

"But if Lord Tam attacked them why haven't they tried to get back here to help? They have to know you are in danger," Rose asked.

"Maybe they can't get back," Mark suggested.

"Why not?"

"These are excellent questions. But the real question is can we get to this place and back before my crystal turns black?" Luke asked.

"Hey, you made a rhyme, Luke!" Peter said.

Luke glared at his little brother. "We need to concentrate, Peter."

Peter's cheeks turned red, and he crossed his arms clearly not willing to participate anymore. Patch licked Peter's head, so Peter leaned into him.

"Meriwether, can we take the puzzle with us and return from where we are?" Mark asked.

"I do not know if the magic lies within me or in the

dragons. As you know, I cannot leave, but if the magic is with them, then wherever they are you may travel through the puzzle." Meriwether said. "Let us take the puzzle to the arena while you train with the dragons. Leave enough time so that if it does not work, you can get back into the castle."

"Could it send us into something like a black hole?" Mark asked. At Meriwether's confused expression, he said, "Like an empty place, no where."

Before Meriwether could respond, Luke said, "I don't think so, Mark. Maybe we'll be in a slightly different spot like what happened to me, but what we are doing is very important to this time and place. We wouldn't be able to travel like this if we weren't really needed."

Mark nodded with a worried face, but he trusted Luke, and they did give their word. They made their way back to the arena and with the puzzle on a table in the corner, the four of them worked on climbing in the saddles onto their dragons' backs. Patch was very ticklish and every time Peter stepped into the stirrup, his foot pressed into Patch's side making him chuckle. His body vibrated, knocking Peter off.

"Patch, you need to stop laughing," Peter said, but the laughter was infectious, so he joined in. When they calmed down, Peter stepped back a few paces, ran toward his dragon and, like a pole-vaulter, launched onto his back. "We did it!" Peter chimed as Patch giggled again.

Rose managed to scramble onto Sparkle's back. Sparkle shook, spraying water onto Rose, but she didn't mind. She made a mental note to wear her bathing suit under her clothes whenever they visited. Otherwise her clothes would always be soaked during their training.

Boulder stood like a model waiting to be painted. Mark pulled himself up onto Boulder's back easily enough, but had to wipe his hands on his jeans since his palms were covered with charcoal from his dragon's scales. Mark quickly opened his sketchpad and drew Boulder with a thin blanket lining his back. *That should take care of any future mess,* Mark thought.

Norris was at the far end of the arena, pumping his wings wide like a peacock and expanding his chest like a rooster. Luke could tell Norris liked to show off. "All right, big guy," Luke said walking toward him. "It's time for you to show me what you can do." Not waiting for another word Norris launched toward Luke with his snout low to the ground. Without any effort, Norris flicked Luke up into the air and seamlessly caught him in his saddle. The bulky dragon stood on his hind legs and bellowed a challenge to the world. Luke laughed as he held on. Norris was just about to set flight when Shimmer's bellow let the wind out of his wings. The enormous dragon, not much smaller than his mother, had the smarts to look sorry. He spun his head around to nuzzle Luke's leg. Luke patted his head. "You just need to be a little calmer, but I understand your enthusiasm."

"Well, that was most impressive," Meriwether said. "Keeping low to the ground, give the command for your dragon to take flight using the word 'fly.'"

They did and like an overgrown carousel the four flew in a circle one way and then the other. Using straps to change directions and speed, the kids lost track of time when Luke said, "It's time to go!"

Immediately, the dragons descended upon the command 'ground' and the kids slid off.

Meriwether hugged each of them. When she came to Luke she said, "Sir Luke. Remember what I said." She smiled, but her eyes held a sadness that Luke thought was because they were leaving.

"I know. We'll be back in two days." He said this, but felt uneasy.

They said quick goodbyes and gathered by the puzzle. "What did Meriwether want you to remember?" Peter asked Luke.

Luke didn't look at his brother. He said, "Everything is fine. We need to go."

Peter didn't press it, but knew his brother was hiding something. Their basement looked the same and when they placed their hands on the puzzle, they returned to their world.

That Sunday, Mark and Rose begged their parents to bring them over to Luke and Peter's house. Luke showed Mark his new *Yu-Gi-Oh* cards that he placed in clear sheet protectors. He wanted to see how many he could collect and enjoyed playing a card game with them. No one liked to play games against Luke because he was a mastermind at strategy. He could see three steps ahead in *Chess* or *Stratego*. His favorite game was *Samurai* and only his mom had the patience to play with him. He'd beat her in a few hands, and they'd start over again.

"Guys, are you ready?" Rose asked impatient to see Sparkle again. She wore her tie-dye blue one-piece bathing suit under her yoga pants and t-shirt. She also put on her sweatshirt with rhinestones. It may not be as glamorous as what Meriwether wore, but Rose knew she could never go wrong with some bling.

Carefully unrolling the puzzle, Peter took the piece out of his pocket. He was terrified he would lose it so he kept it in a locked blue metal box on his dresser. Everyone gathered around the puzzle they set up in the tree house, which Luke and Peter built with their dad in the backyard. When Peter placed the piece into its proper place it glowed, and they ended up outside the castle walls by the entrance to the forest. Shimmer and her dragons waited for them. A page held the puzzle in a box.

Luke said, "Mount your dragons and let's go inside the castle."

The page climbed onto Shimmer's back after placing the puzzle in a satchel, and they flew to the open arena. Patch stumbled a little while landing launching Peter over his head. Luckily, Patch was fast and caught him before he hit the ground.

"You need to pay attention and hang on, Peter," Luke said. "I don't want you getting hurt."

"I know!" Peter said, mad his brother still thought he could treat him like a baby even though Luke was only two years older. Peter was going into fifth grade for crying out loud.

"I see the puzzle worked. As we know that the magic is with the dragons, you can now travel further. It is time for you to train on how to ride and fight."

They all wore chain mail, and Peter slipped his bow and arrow across his shoulders as Luke sheathed his sword.

"Sir Mark, although your pencil is a mighty weapon, I feel you must have something else." She handed him a stick that was covered in black leather, but had a hard ball at one end.

Mark stared at it not knowing what he was supposed to do. As he was raised to be polite, he said, "Uh, thanks, Meriwether."

The princess laughed and asked, "Would you like to know what it does?"

"It does something?" Mark asked not meaning to be funny, but everyone laughed as they gathered closer.

"Not too close," Meriwether warned. Taking the stick from Mark, she pressed a button at the bottom and the stick became taller than Mark.

"Wow!" Rose exclaimed. "That's cool."

Mark thought it was rather uncanny that he had just started Bo staff lessons at his karate school and knew a few things about the weapon. He took it from Meriwether's outstretched hand, twisted it in front of him, and whipped it over each shoulder, getting the feel of the weapon.

"Press the button again to close it," Meriwether said.

Knowing that Rose was showing great restraint not asking what her weapon was, Meriwether handed her a thick rope with a ball attached to each end.

"What is it?" Rose asked.

"It's a bola," Luke said.

"That's great, but what am I supposed to do with it?"

"You hold onto the middle of the rope, swing it around your head, and throw it at your enemy. The balls are hard enough to knock your enemy out or you can trip them by throwing it at their legs. It's a very effective weapon and with your accuracy in basketball, it's perfect for you."

Rose beamed and put the weapon in her pouch.

They each hopped onto their dragons' backs, fully armored, weapons at the ready. Shimmer flew into the sky ahead of them and flipped and soared. Her dragons followed their mother and soon glided behind her copying every move.

Just as Rose said, "This is fun!" Shimmer flipped midair and her dragons did the same. Peter fell off Patch, held on tight with one hand and was saved when his dragon flipped back over.

"That was close!" Mark yelled, his normal calm demeanor evaporating with fear.

"Shimmer says to squeeze your knees together," Luke said.

Peter muttered under his breath, wondering why no one else fell out of the saddle. As Patch swayed back and forth, Peter swayed with him and realized it wasn't much different than riding a dirt bike. Then he remembered watching Travis Pastrana do a double flip on his dirt bike. Pastrana would arch his back and lean into the flip. The momentum kept his legs in place, so maybe pushing on the pegs helped. Peter tightened the stirrups hoping his feet wouldn't fall out again.

Luke wondered if this was the first part of the riddle or if the ride to the gathering would be like a roller coaster ride. Would it be dangerous; would they make it there in one day? Would he be strong enough to do whatever had to be done to reunite Meriwether with her parents and Shimmer with her mate? The start of school was only three days away. Yes, Luke's wish was to make it to the first day of school, but he wanted to do it whole. He dreaded explaining to classmates why he didn't have any hair on his head. He didn't think he could take people looking at him with pity. Luke only wanted to be treated like a normal kid.

Luke shook off any fear or doubts and rode on the back of Norris getting a feel for how the dragon turned and anticipated his movements. Luke was in the moment, excited to be so high in the sky free of all worries—except for falling off, he guessed. Luke knew that Norris would save him. He heard Shimmer's voice in his head and yelled the command 'ground.' Everyone landed in the arena.

"How did you fare?" Meriwether asked as she passed around mugs of water.

They drank deeply not realizing how physically exhausting it was riding a dragon.

"Besides the fact that we almost lost Peter, it was fantastic!" Rose replied.

"I had it under control," Peter grumbled not wanting to be the center of attention for screwing up.

"That is how we learn, Sir Peter. You will never make the same mistake again. Would you agree?" Meriwether said.

Peter shrugged his shoulders and said, "No, I guess not."

After a short break, Meriwether started dragon sparring drills. This involved riding on their dragons and attacking a stationary target with their weapons. Luke went first. He drew his sword and had a hard time keeping his sword still as Norris' steps shook him like an elephant. He laughed because his Poppa always said that Luke's mom walked like an elephant going up and down the stairs.

"Norris, try to walk smoother. Don't stomp, glide." Luke pictured himself smoothly moving along the dojo floor in karate and felt the shift in Norris' step. Luke's eyebrow shot up. *"You could see what I pictured in my head?"*

Norris bellowed so Luke took that as a yes. *This could come in very handy for communication,* Luke thought. Now that it was easier to see the target, Luke practiced leaning forward and toward the right so he could reach the pile of hay that had a face painted on it. A few times his sword stuck in the hay, and Luke tried not to think about the possibility of having to really stab someone with his sword. He did it often enough in his video games, but he knew the difference between that and real life.

Rose went next. She hadn't had time to practice with her bola and then a thought occurred to her. "Meriwether, how am I going to get my weapon back? I only have one shot. If I miss, I'm in big trouble."

Meriwether smiled and petted Sparkle's side as she peered up at Rose. "Your bola is very special. Can you snap your fingers?"

"Sure," Rose said and snapped her fingers on both hands.

"Excellent. Throw your bola at one of the poles."

Carefully folding her bola in half, Rose held onto the rope with one hand. With one eye closed and her tongue sticking out of her mouth, Rose swung it over her head and let loose. The bola missed the pole and hit the wall behind it.

"That was terrible!" Rose said.

"Snap your fingers once," Meriwether said ignoring Rose's criticism of herself.

Breathing out in frustration, Rose snapped her finger and the bola appeared in her hand. "Way cool," Rose said. "How did it do that?"

Meriwether said, "It is connected to you and will always find its way back now that you have thrown it. Why don't you and Sparkle go to the far wall and practice your aim."

It was Peter's turn. He had strong legs and solid stomach muscles. He thought about the *Robin Hood* movie where one of the merry men stood on his horse to shoot a bow and arrow. As Patch stepped forward, Peter stood in his stirrups keeping his core and leg muscles tight. Taking a deep breath he pulled back the string on his bow and hit the target. It was the outermost ring, but he still hooted with success. He retrieved the arrow and took a few more turns with Patch moving faster and faster. It was easy on the ground. The real test would be in the air.

Finally, it was Mark's turn. Mark had taken the time to draw some attack forms with his Bo staff. When he was done with a few moves on separate pages he flipped through and could see the stick figures flow through the motions of the full technique. Even though he would be on Boulder's back, the upper body movements would be the same. There were melons on top of hay bales on both sides of him. Closing his eyes, Mark pictured the staff as an extension of his arm and knocked the melons off. When Mark first began karate and had to spar, his body felt like it would shut down, and he became so frustrated because he couldn't remember any of the techniques. Instructor Adam taught him how to visualize the technique all the way to scoring a point.

"Let's do this, Boulder," Mark said tapping his dragon on the back. Boulder moved like he weighed a ton, but a few taps from Mark got him moving a bit faster. *Luckily he can fly fast,* Mark thought. They'd never have a chance otherwise. Mark swung the staff in a downward arc to his left knocking the melon clean off the bale and then seamlessly hitting the melon on his right. He pierced the smiling hay bale that Luke had stabbed earlier and then twirled the staff above his head like a propeller. It caused the dirt on the ground to stir and the other kids had to shut their eyes.

"Stop it, Mark!" Peter yelled, and Mark lowered his staff.

"That was fantastic," Luke said slapping his friend on his back. "Let's go over the plan one more time before we have to leave."

Peter groaned, "We know everything already."

"One can never know strategy too well, and it is vital that you look at every angle before going into battle," Meriwether said.

Rose still couldn't believe they were preparing for battle. She likened it to training for basketball tryouts or qualifying for swimming. You set a goal and trained your body to be the best it could be. Rose knew that playing sports was just as much a mental game as it was physical (sometimes more, her dad always told her) and to be honest she knew she struggled with that. She was never certain if she had what it took to win. She played and made the best teams, but what happened if she didn't grow or wasn't as strong and lagged behind? Could she catch up?

"Rose, are you listening?" Mark asked, interrupting her thoughts.

"What? Oh yes," she said. Rose wouldn't let her team down. For that's what they were: a team. And as what happened with most teams, they became a family. The four of them had always been a family for as long as Rose could remember. She loved Peter and Luke like they were her own siblings. It was strange and heartwarming that her family had grown to include a gorgeous medieval princess and adorably beautiful dragons. No one would ever believe her.

"The next time we come back, we will fly over the Arcadian Mountains with our dragons in search of the gathering. When we get there, we'll hopefully find some willing knights who will help us save the king."

Rose interrupted, "Do any of the other kingdoms have dragons?"

Meriwether thought. "I do not know. Dragons are supposed to be able to sense one another, but we are so far removed, Shimmer has not noticed. Plus, she and Copper have not been a part of another dragon family in a very long time. They may not accept your dragons."

Luke said, "It's too bad Shimmer can't come with us, but

I understand she needs to be here with you." Luke checked his crystal. "We have to leave!"

After saying goodbye to Meriwether and the dragons, the kids touched the puzzle. Luke let out a cry. Even though they all had their hands on the puzzle, his form lingered for a moment. Meriwether stared in horror as his body appeared to be caught in between worlds. Luke flickered one more time. Then he was gone.

Rose, Peter, and Mark fell over one another in the cramped tree house.

"This is the last time we travel from this tree house. It's too small!" Peter said and then gasped.

Luke's body appeared and then faded out like the end of a home video. Rose reached for him and, when he looked solid, grabbed his wrist and pulled. Luke fell on her out of breath.

"What happened?" Mark asked kneeling.

His friend didn't respond.

"Something's wrong. Get your mom, Peter," Mark said.

Peter didn't wait to be asked twice. He catapulted down the yellow slide and ran toward the house screaming for his mom.

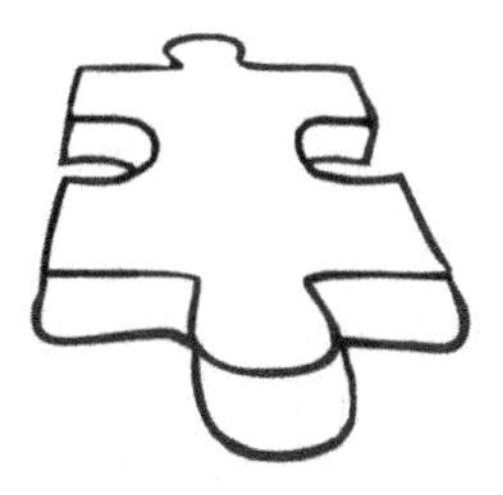

Chapter Twelve

Luke lay in the hospital bed. Peter's mom said he had a tough night and was in a lot of pain. The doctors had given him some medicine to help him sleep. When the doctor arrived and asked to talk to his parents, Peter said he would watch over his brother. Pulling a chair close to Luke, Peter took out his *Pokemon* character *Charizard* and curled Luke's fingers around it. He knew how Luke always liked to have something in his hands and maybe it would help. Peter was mad that he didn't know how sick his brother really was. From the look on his parents' face, Peter knew time was running out for his biggest hero.

The next day, Rose and Mark came to the hospital with their parents to visit Luke. He was eating his lunch and was watching *A Tale of Despereaux* movie with Peter. It was a fitting story for heroes on a quest.

Rose rushed to Luke's side and hugged him. "Oh, Luke! We were so scared for you! When you didn't come back right away . . . ."

"Shhh," her brother scolded.

"Sorry," Rose whispered, tears rolling down her pale cheeks.

"Mom," Luke started.

"What do you need?"

"Maybe Rachel and Sam would like to take you and Dad to the café and have some lunch. I'm sure you have a lot to catch up on, and then we can watch the movie."

Luke's mom beamed at him through her sadness. "You're a sweetie. Are you sure?" she asked looking at each of them.

They all nodded with fake smiles on their faces, but Luke's mom was too tired to notice.

"All right, but we won't be long."

"Why didn't you tell us you were getting worse, Luke?" Peter asked. "We would have done things differently."

Luke tried to squeeze Peter's arm. "Like what, Peter? Would you not have hung out with me, not gone on vacation, not have been an annoying little brother," he joked trying to lighten the mood.

Mark spoke, "We're not sure, but would have liked some honesty."

"I really don't know how sick I am. I wouldn't have wanted to be treated any other way, and we have always truly lived whether we were having fun together or fighting. I want the fighting and the arguing. It makes me feel normal. What really makes me feel normal is this quest, which doesn't make sense, as there is nothing normal about it! Shimmer told me that Lord Tam is gathering an army of warriors from neighboring kingdoms. Somehow he has turned them against Meriwether's father, claiming he is the one behind night attacks on the villages. We know Tam is the attacker," Luke said.

"How can we go? You are so sick, Luke," Mark said in a quiet voice.

Luke took in their sad and worried faces. He scrunched

his face in determination and said, "Look, we made a commitment to help others who are in need, and we can't let them down now. It's not about me anymore."

"Who's going to help you?" Rose asked. "You give and give, Luke. You're the first one to go out of your way to help another person, but now you are in trouble. I'm afraid for you!" Rose said and fell across Luke's chest crying.

Luke patted Rose's shoulder, upset that his condition made her cry. There was so much he still wanted to do, and he felt like his time was short. Yes, he wanted his wish. He wanted to get back to school, but this quest was bigger than all of them. Besides, he gave his word, and that was not something he would break.

"Do you remember when I first got this rash, Rose?"

Rose lifted her head and nodded. Peter handed her a tissue, and she wiped her face.

"I was better when I traveled to the dragons. We can still do this. The time is now, but we have to do this together. I can't do it without each of you." He held his hand out palm down like a team huddle. Mark was the first to place his hand over Luke's. Then Rose placed her small hand on top of her brother's. Luke looked at his little brother. "Peter? Are you with me? We need you to finish this with us."

Peter nodded and placed his hand on top of the others. A huge lump formed in his throat, but he would be brave for Luke.

"I knew I could count on all of you. Peter, do you have the puzzle?" Luke asked.

"Right here." Peter pulled the rolled green felt out of his backpack. Luke shuffled to the side of his bed. He wore his long sleeve Yankees shirt and warm up pants. After putting on his sneakers, he said, "Let's do this."

Peter placed the piece, and the friends flew off to a land where they had a chance to make a difference.

When they landed in the arena, Luke was on his knees with his face in his hands. Everyone was stone silent, worried that the trip had made Luke worse. Slowly, Luke placed one foot on the ground, then the other, and stood. His brown curly hair shone like he just shampooed it, his face was round and full of color, and he had a bounce in his step. His smile lit up everyone's world, and they all cheered.

Then Mark frowned. "I don't understand why you are so much better here. What does it mean?"

Concerned, Meriwether asked, "Have you not gotten better, Sir Luke?"

Luke had mind-spoke with Norris and Shimmer, but he sugarcoated how sick he was. They had enough to worry about.

"I'm fine, but am much better here," he answered.

Meriwether only nodded like she saw much more than Luke told her. "Then let us hurry. I have placed the puzzle in Norris' sack. Give yourself enough time to return." Meriwether petted Shimmer's back, fighting to keep her emotions under control. "Shimmer's dragons will stay wherever you end up, so that you will go back to them. Find a safe hiding place when you have to leave. Come as often as you can and please be careful."

She hugged each of them before they climbed on their dragons' backs. Hugging the dragons, Meriwether gently cried thinking that young and unseasoned warriors were doing what she should have been doing. They had trained hard, and she could only hope that they would bring her parents and the knights back to the castle in time. All she could do was wait and keep her kingdom safe.

Shimmer nudged each one of her dragons and mind-spoke to Luke.

"I know, girl. We'll make sure we all get back safe."

They flew over the forest watching for trollics or flying arrows and soon reached the Arcadian Mountains.

Luke yelled over the wind to Mark. "Does that look like a rollercoaster to you?" The mountains rose high into the sky and plummeted to deep valleys.

Mark replied, "Yeah! I guess it was literal, but do we need to fly through it like a rollercoaster or can we just fly over it?"

Rose answered their question when she flew to the top of the highest peak and landed.

"Why did you stop?" Peter asked.

Rose waved her hand at them to be quiet. "Do you hear that?"

They shook their heads, but Sparkle and the other dragons appeared distressed.

"It sounds like a cow in pain!" Rose said. "Peter, start humming."

Peter scowled. "Rose, I hum to dragons, not cows."

Rose gave him that look and Peter hummed, '*When the Saints Go Marching In.*' Rose almost gave him another look, but the sound eased.

Peter checked his watch's GPS and saw a white dot in the upper right corner. "I think I know where it is," Peter said.

"But are we supposed to find it? Is it dangerous?" Mark asked.

"He's scared, not dangerous," Rose said. "I know it."

By now the boys knew not to question Rose's intuition.

"Lead the way, Peter," Luke said.

Peter whispered to Patch, "Do you see the worn path

on the mountains? We need to follow it as closely as possible." Patch snorted so Peter took that as a yes. He shifted in his saddle and said, "It'll be like follow the leader so just follow me as close as you can. You'll see the path as we go."

Not knowing what awaited him, Peter nudged Patch forward and off the edge of the mountain. The path down the mountain was like a water slide, but it was packed dirt with very low ridges on each side. Patch glided down the steep slope and managed to stay on the path. As they neared the valley, Patch did a 360 and flapped his wings toward the top of the next slope. Peter concentrated hard on staying on his dragon and hoped that his brother and friends hung on, too. It was like the Boomerang rollercoaster ride at the theme park up in Lake George. Peter hoped they wouldn't have to go backwards.

After the second descent Patch shot up and spun over backwards like they had practiced. Peter leaned back, tightened his legs around his dragon, and enjoyed the ride.

Luke let out a whoop and Peter responded with laughter. At the bottom of the third mountain peak, Patch quickly veered to the right and stopped short in front of an opening in the mountain.

"Not another cave!" Peter moaned.

The other dragons stopped by Patch. Peter hummed and the moaning began in earnest.

"Do you have any idea why we need to get whatever that is?" Luke asked Rose.

Rose thought for a moment. "It has something to do with finding dragons and gold."

"And it's getting anxious! I think something else big and scary is trying to find it!" Peter urged.

"The dragons can't fit in the opening. How about if two

of us go in and two stay here?" Luke suggested.

Peter said, "I need to go so it can hear my humming."

"Makes sense. Who do you think should go with you?"

"I think Rose since she sensed the creature in the first place. That will make it quicker to find."

Mark objected. "I don't know about the two of you going in there alone."

"Mark, I am just as able to take care of myself as is Peter or either of you!" Rose said.

"I know, but I can't let anything happen to you. I'm worried, Rose. It has nothing to do with your ability to protect yourself," Mark said.

Rose huffed not believing him. She crossed her arms and turned away.

Mark threw his hands up in the air and slid off of Boulder. The others did the same.

"I agree with Mark. It's our job as your older siblings to look after you no matter how old you get. Just watch each other's backs and whistle if you need help. Use the light on your phone or your watch."

Peter notched an arrow in his bow. "Ready, Rose?"

She nodded. "Rose," Mark started.

Rose gave her brother a half smile and kissed him on the cheek. "I know, Mark. I'll be careful."

Mark nodded and withdrew his Bo staff just in case. Luke stood next to his best friend, sword unsheathed ready to guard Rose and Peter against anything going in or coming out.

Rose turned on her phone's flashlight and aimed it in front of her as Peter followed humming *'The Star Spangled Banner.'* "He seems to like patriotic songs," Peter whispered.

Rose giggled, but stopped when she heard the moans.

"I think he's this way."

The moans stopped when Rose's flashlight caught a pair of red eyes. She almost dropped the phone, but let out her breath when the moans came out of the mouth connected to the red eyes. It took a moment for Rose to understand what she was looking at. It was about a foot tall with ears and a trunk like an elephant. Its body was round and mostly gray with a white spot on the belly.

"What is that?" Peter asked.

At Peter's voice, it lifted its trunk and moaned mournfully. Rose shone the flashlight around him and realized he was stuck.

"Oh you poor thing! He's stuck, Peter!"

Peter tried to remember the words to the *'Star Spangled Banner'* since that seemed to calm the animal down. "O say can you see."

The animal stopped moaning and looked at Peter with scared eyes. At least they looked scared to Peter. He sure hoped that was it and not how this animal looked before it ripped someone's face off.

Peter had never been a fan of animals. He actually was afraid of them. It was kind of hilarious that Patch didn't bother him at all, but Peter figured they had a deep connection. Luke loved animals and had a hamster named Chipper at home. Luke carried Chipper around and let it run around his room while he did homework. Peter had a hamster named Zippy, but Luke was always the one to hold it. Peter so wanted to be like his big brother, but Luke had some very big shoes to fill. He should have been the one in here, not Peter. Peter was tired of being afraid and unsure.

Rose's voice cut into his thoughts. "Peter, this little guy needs us. Keep singing and try to lift the rock on his paw."

Peter stepped closer and saw that a good-sized rock had trapped the animal. It was in pain. "By the dawn's early light." Peter sang and smiled at it. The finder (as Rose decided to call it) stopped moaning and watched. "What so proudly we hailed at the twilight's last gleaming?" Peter squatted, wrapped his arms around the rock and lifted.

"Got him!" Rose said hastily grabbing the animal without thinking of the consequences. The finder wrapped his arms and legs around Rose like a koala bear and sniffed her hair with his trunk. "He's so adorable and soft!"

Peter held out his hand and the finder sniffed it and sneezed. Slime covered Peter's hand. "Gross!" he said and wiped his hand on a nearby rock. The finder tucked its head in Rose's neck and shut its eyes. "Let's get out of here," Peter said and Rose followed. They exited the cave. Luke and Mark hurried over to them.

"Hey there, little guy," Mark said petting its head.

"Nice job, you two," Luke said. "What's his name?"

Peter and Rose glanced at one another and said, "Finder," at the same time. Everyone laughed.

"Well let's see if he can help us find the volcano of gold," Mark said. He withdrew his sketchbook from his satchel and drew a gold nugget. It appeared in his hand.

Rose gave it to Finder. He grasped it in his little paws, sniffed and licked it. "Find the gold, Finder," Rose said and pointed from the gold nugget to the dragons. Finder lifted his trunk in the air and whimpered toward Sparkle. "You want to get on the dragon?" Rose asked.

Finder whimpered again. They hopped on their dragons and flew toward the direction Finder pointed with his trunk. They flew for what seemed like hours, and as the sky began to darken so did Luke's crystal.

He flew over them and yelled, "We have to find shelter for the dragons and head home!"

They landed near a forest and quickly searched for some coverage for four large dragons that were still considered babies and Finder who seemed just as young.

"If they need our help so much why do they have this rule that we have to get back so quickly?" Rose asked. "This will be impossible!"

"I don't know, Rose," Luke said. "It's just my job to get us back safely." Luke mind-spoke to Norris. *"You have to make sure that everyone stays hidden in this area. There are bad people who will hurt you."*

"What will they eat?" Peter asked.

"They'll find something," Luke said.

Rose put Finder down next to Sparkle. "You need to stay here with the dragons. We'll be back in a couple days." Sniffling, Rose hugged Finder then Sparkle.

They removed the puzzle and laid it on the ground behind a tree. There were so many problems that they hadn't thought about. What if something ate the puzzle? What if the dragons took off and left Finder? Some of their anxiety was relieved when Finder sat by the puzzle and cooed happily.

"I think he likes the puzzle," Rose said. "Stay with the puzzle, Finder."

They touched the puzzle and were gone.

They landed in the fun room, which was outside the patient rooms. Luke immediately felt lightheaded, so they grabbed his arms and led him to his room. One of his nurses saw them and pursed her lips. "What are you doing out of your room, young man?"

"Uh, we thought it might be nice to take a walk," Peter said, grinning sheepishly.

Luke smiled weakly and was ushered back to his bed. Peter removed the puzzle piece and quickly rolled it up while Mark and Rose shielded his actions. It was in his backpack before their parents returned. Luke fell asleep as they finished watching the movie. His rash was worse, and he lost all the healthy color and hair he had in the dragon's world.

Before Peter left with his dad, he gave his brother a light peck on his forehead and hugged his mom.

Every summer the brothers usually slept in each other's rooms. Actually, Peter always slept on a sleeping bag next to Luke's bed. Still young enough to hold his dad's hand, Peter took it and asked, "Can I have a sleepover in your room, Dad?"

Squeezing his hand, his dad said, "Sure."

It was time for karate, but Peter didn't feel like going, especially without Luke. This was one of the few times that Peter was at class and Luke wasn't. Usually it was because of sports and not because his big brother was in the hospital.

After his dad bribed him with the promise of an ice cream cone after karate, Peter decided to go. Maybe he'd have a chance to talk to Rose and Mark about the dragons. They would be able to return on Saturday and hopefully Luke would be home. Luke had missed the first three days of school and Peter absolutely would not travel without him. Peter was worried that Luke's part of the wish hadn't come true, but surely after all they had done, Luke would be healed.

Most of the other students in his class were about the same age and everyone was very close. Karate was like another family. They had summer and holiday parties. All the kids gathered around Peter and asked about Luke. Peter knew they were concerned, but he didn't want to think about it. He didn't want to cry.

"Hey, Peter!" Mark called and picking him up around the waist hauled him over to the other side of the room. Peter took a moment to calm down.

Peter slowly put on his uniform as Mark and Rose stood by.

"Any dreams or news of the dragons?" Rose asked.

Peter shook his head. "I didn't sleep well last night, and I haven't had a chance to talk to Luke. I hope he'll be home tomorrow. Then we can go back."

Both siblings nodded feeling lost without Luke and his connection to the dragons.

Instructor Adam yelled, "Line up!"

After jumping jacks and stretches, the students separated into pairs. Peter and Rose hit the heavy bags. "Backhand, reverse punch, rear roundhouse kick!" Instructor Adam kept calling off the punches and kicks. As Peter thought about the dragons, saving Meriwether's family, and how sick and sad his brother looked when Peter had to leave him in the hospital, his punches and kicks got harder and faster. Peter grunted as he pummeled the bag like it was the answer to all his problems. Instructor Adam's large hand on his shoulder stopped him mid-swing and Peter shuddered from the exertion. He didn't think he ever worked so hard. With his instructor blocking the rest of the class, he leaned over and whispered, "Take a deep breath and wipe your face."

Taking the end of his belt Peter wiped the tears he hadn't known were streaming down his face. He felt weak and embarrassed until his instructor said, "The best thing you can do for yourself and your brother is to let it out. Never hold your anger in, because it will backfire when you least want it." He tousled Peter's hair and continued class.

Peter did feel better and found he could concentrate on the self-defense. Class went quickly and at the end, everyone presented him with a big get-well card to bring home for Luke. Peter thanked everyone and the entire class went out for ice cream.

The sun shone warm on Peter's back as he rode his bike up and down his road. His mom had called. She and Luke were on their way home. Peter jumped off the curb and lifted the front end of his bike into a wheelie. He looked forward to dirt biking next weekend and hoped Luke could go with them. Peter heard the horn blare behind him. He spun his bike around. He zipped in behind his mom in the driveway. Throwing his bike on the ground, Peter ran over to Luke's side and opened the door. His smile faded.

Luke gave a worn smile, "Hey, Petey, what's up?"

"Uh, not much. I held my wheelie for five seconds today," Peter replied.

"That's great," Luke said, holding onto Peter as he stood. Their dad came out and gripped Luke in a big bear hug. Then he pulled Peter into it. Luke was already up to their dad's shoulder and Peter barely reached his chest, but he knew he'd shoot up like Luke in a year or so. Some day, he and Luke would be the same size.

As Luke was made comfortable on the couch, the phone rang. Peter answered it. "Hi, Rose. Luke's home!"

"Oh, I'm so glad! My mom wants to bring food over for dinner. Do you think that would be all right?"

Peter asked his mom and said to Rose, "Yup, she says that would be nice. Are you and Mark coming over?"

"Of course, Silly! So get the you know what ready."

"I will. Plus, I think it will be good for Luke. He doesn't look so hot."

"Oh, Peter. I'm sorry. I should have asked how Luke was doing the minute I got you on the phone."

"That's OK. He said he wanted to be treated like normal. As a matter of fact, I'm going to try my hardest to annoy him. See you soon!"

Rose laughed and hung up. Peter thought it felt good to laugh and asked Luke if he wanted to watch *Beverly Hills Chihuahua*. Luke agreed, so they went downstairs. His brother was soon laughing and Peter loved the sound.

Two hours later Luke slept on the couch as Peter played video games. He heard the door to the basement open and nudged Luke. Luke asked to be awakened as soon as his friends arrived, so Peter did just that.

Rose rushed over and hugged Luke and then Peter. Then she gushed out her words. "I had a dream about Finder last night. He was in a pile of gold. I think Copper and Meriwether's parents have moved and are at the volcano!"

"We'd better hurry then," Luke said. "Peter, get my bag."

Peter handed over the camouflage colored bag that had a picture of the world on it. Luke used it for his Game Boy and other items he held throughout the day. He took out his crystal and placed it around his neck.

"That's the first I saw you without that, Luke," Peter said.

"Yeah, well with the doctors poking and prodding me, I didn't want anyone to ask questions or take it off and lose it."

Peter dragged the puzzle out from under a table and unlocked his safe. "Here we go," he said and placed the piece. The puzzle changed to solid gold and the friends placed their hands on the puzzle, hoping they were ready.

They fell on something hard and the sun reflected gold all around them. Not the sun, Luke decided as he stood. Everything was solid gold, including the trees, ground and the magnificent volcano looming in front of them. A vast amount of water was all they could see for miles.

"Is the volcano on an island?" Mark asked.

"There's only one way to find out. Let's go this way," Luke waved and walked around big boulders.

Everyone followed and soon they found their dragons. Finder sat curled under Sparkle's wing and tooted his trunk in excitement at seeing them. Peter picked up the little creature and Finder hung on for dear life.

"Poor guy is shaking," Peter said.

"Maybe he's cold. Hand him over," Rose said. "Mark, can you make one of those baby carriers? It might make it easier to keep track of him and he'll be warm against one of our bodies."

Mark shook his head, but drew a baby sling. After Rose tucked Finder in, he cuddled up close, but pointed his trunk toward the volcano.

"What do you think he's trying to tell us?" Mark asked.

Luke had his arm around Norris and was listening intently, even though no one else could hear them. "Thanks, Norris," he said, and shifted his attention to the others. "Finder seems to think that the king and his knights are trapped inside the volcano."

"Is there a way inside?" Rose asked. "It's not too big. Maybe we can see if there is an opening."

"If there is then why can't they get out?" Peter asked.

"Good question, Peter. Let's fly our dragons around the volcano starting at the bottom and look for any openings. If it's dormant and the opening is big enough, maybe we can fly inside," Luke said. "Then we'll also know if this is an island."

They hopped on their dragons and flew around slowly. The volcano was smooth and shiny with some crevasses where the gold must have bubbled and hardened.

"This must be worth a fortune!" Peter yelled.

They circled the top and saw an opening. As they flew closer, something dark covered the sun. Looking up, Luke barely had time to react and screamed, "Dragon! Get inside the volcano!"

Not checking to see if they could fit, they skydived into the opening. Mark furiously drew headlamps for all of them and as they roughly landed, turned his on and tossed the rest to the others.

"Keep them off for a second," Luke said.

"But it's so dark," Rose said in a shaky voice.

"I know, but I'm not sure if whoever attacked can see us, and I don't want to give them a target."

They didn't have to wait long to find out what would happen next. "Salutations! This was almost too easy," Lord Tam called from the top of the mountain. "It's too bad Shimmer isn't here too, but that won't matter. I already have her mate and once I marry Princess Meriwether, Shimmer will be mine to control and then our lands will finally be united."

"We'll just wait until you leave and fly out of here!" Rose yelled.

"I'm afraid not. I've prepared for this moment, and you are not getting back out. I'll give the princess your regards." With that they heard a loud grating sound and slowly the light above them got smaller and smaller until they were left in complete darkness.

Rose screamed, but then calmed down when everyone turned on the headlights.

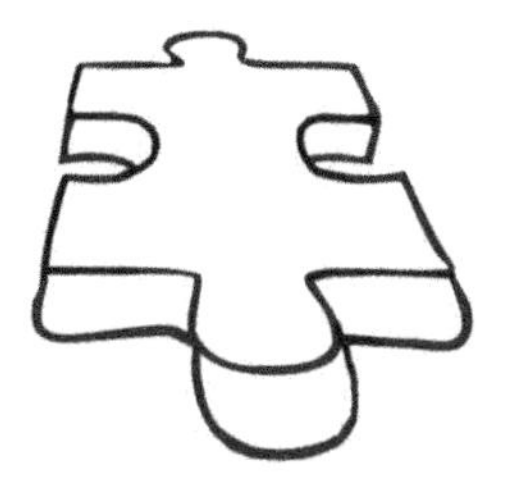

Chapter Thirteen

"Now what, Luke?" Peter hoped his brother had a plan.

Luke peered around him. It looked as though someone had been mining in there for years. "Let's look for Copper. Lord Tam already told us they are here, so let's find them and figure out why Copper couldn't fly them out."

"Maybe the top was on there before. He opened the top and forced us in. We fell for his trap," Mark said shaking his head.

"Hey, we're only kids," Peter exclaimed. "We can't help that we're gullible."

"We may be gullible, but we aren't defenseless," Luke said. "Let's follow this opening and see where it leads."

They heard people whispering and trying to be quiet. Luke raised his arm and everyone stopped. It reminded Peter of the soldiers in some of their video games. His brother was a natural leader. Peter was proud of Luke and happy he was back to his regular self. Peter didn't think about when they had to go home.

Luke planned to address the king and queen, but he turned to the group and whispered, "What are their names? Meriwether never told us!"

They all stared at each other, not believing they could have missed something so basic!

Names didn't matter at this point. Getting out of there did. Luke began, "Hello! We come in peace!"

Peter snickered behind him, and Luke swatted at him to shut him up.

"We come in the name of Princess Meriwether as knights sworn to save you! Do not be afraid!" Luke said, hoping he sounded official.

A bellowing voice commanded, "If you are a knight, then show yourself."

"Let's go." Luke led the way, and the four of them rounded the corner. Finder shook in Rose's sling and snorted when he saw all the people.

Luke knelt and motioned for the three of them to do the same. The king motioned for them to rise. When they did, he spoke, "I am King Alfred Drasnor of Castle Dragonia. This is my wife, Queen Thelia. Who are you?"

Luke said, "I am Sir Luke. This is my brother, Sir Peter and our friends Sir Mark and Lady Rose. The little animal with Rose is Finder. He led us to you."

The king looked at them and didn't seem very happy. "My daughter must think very highly of you to send you on this quest, but she may have been foolish to think that four mere youths could get us out of here."

At his comment, Luke smiled. "We aren't alone. Norris!" he called.

With that Norris, Boulder, Patch, and Sparkle clomped into the room. Their presence shook the king. "Whose dragons are these?"

Peter spoke, "These are Shimmer and Copper's babies. We saved them when they were eggs, bonded with them when they hatched, and are trained to ride them." Peter looked around. "But where is Copper? I'm sure they want to meet their dad."

At the mention of Copper's name, the king's face fell. "I do not know where Copper is. When they imprisoned us in the volcano, they chained Copper and hauled him away. He may not be alive."

"That's horrible!" Rose said. "Shimmer will be heartbroken. How will we get everyone home?"

"And about that. We had better hurry. Lord Tam is going to force Princess Meriwether, uh your daughter, to marry him. He turned one of the dragons bad and plans to take over your kingdom. Um, your highness, Sir." Mark stopped speaking, as he didn't want to start stuttering on top of rambling on. The seriousness of the situation was making him very anxious.

"By Gods! We have to get out of here!" the king said.

At the king's shouting, Finder squirmed so Rose let him out of his sling. Finder sniffed around and tooted like he did the last time he found something.

"What is it, Finder?" Rose asked. She bent down close to a gold wall and touched the ground. "It's water flowing through the wall. I wonder where it's coming from?" Rose absently rubbed Finder's head, and he rolled over onto his back. "So you want a belly rub as a reward?" She laughed and petted his belly.

"I noticed a stream where the gold ended. Maybe it's coming from there," Peter said.

"If water can get in here, then maybe there's a way for us to get out," Luke said. He turned to Mark. "What would be the best way to make a hole in a wall made of gold?"

Mark thought about a movie he had seen that past

winter about drilling a hole to the center of the earth. The drill looked like an oversized screw. He took his sketchpad out of his bag and sitting against Boulder began to draw. Mark was about to stand and show everyone his idea when Boulder's front claw reached over his shoulder. With his claw, he added two handles on the back end. Shaking his head in disbelief, Mark said, "You are one smart dragon."

"Did Boulder just draw with you?" Rose asked.

"He did, and I think the drill is ready to operate. Everyone move away from the wall." As they stepped back, they all looked at the drill and imagined it life-size in front of them. The drill appeared just as easily as Peter's hamburger had the first time.

At the sight of the machine, the king shoved his wife behind him and demanded, "What sort of magic do you practice?"

His knights had drawn closer with suspicion and menace.

"Allow me to explain, King Drasnor," Luke began. "We are not from your land, nor of your time. Princess Meriwether summoned us, because she believed we had the skills and powers to save your kingdom. Our magic is from Shimmer's scales and has served us well."

Shimmer's magic was something the king could understand. He rubbed his long beard and asked, "What do you plan to do with this?"

Luke motioned to Mark who stepped forward. "Well, it will turn and drill a hole into the wall. The water at the base of the wall indicates that it may not be that thick. We are hoping we can make a hole big enough to get through. I have the ability to make my drawings come to life, which is what I just did."

The king still looked shocked, but his need to escape

helped him recover quickly. "That is fine, then. What can we do to help?"

"If two of your stronger knights could help push the drill forward as it turns, that would make it go faster," Mark said.

King Drasnor summoned his strongest knights.

Luke said, "Let's position it above the spot where water is trickling in."

With the help of Norris, they managed to move the drill close enough to the wall. Mark primed the engine, then pressed a button to start it. After all, if he was going to draw a tool, he may as well make it easy to operate. It was very loud. They hoped it didn't attract their enemies, but it couldn't be helped. They had to get out and find a way to get everyone back to the castle.

The knights grabbed the two handles and pushed their weight against it. As the drill touched the wall and spun, flecks of gold shot at everyone. "Shield your eyes!" Mark yelled and threw goggles he had drawn to them.

Sparkle didn't like the chips of gold and began to shake like a dog next to the drill. "Sparkle!" Rose yelled over the noise. "What are you doing?"

Water flew from her scales and coated the drill and the wall. The gold fell to the ground instead of shooting at them. "You're a smart dragon, too," Rose said smiling.

The wall shook and shafts of light poked through the cavern. "We did it!" Peter called. "You'll need to make it a little bigger so the dragons can get out."

They backed up the drill, moved it a little to the right and started again. About an hour later the hole was big enough for Norris.

Luke sat on a golden rock and rolled clumps of wet gold in his hand. The heat from the drill combined with the water softened it enough so that he could make little figures with the material. Everyone knew that when Luke was working with his hands he was in his own world thinking. So they waited.

Finally, he stood and handed Rose a mermaid made of gold. "Oh Luke! It's beautiful! How did you do that?"

Luke shrugged. "I don't know. For some reason, mermaids came into my mind. Maybe because of Sparkle and all the water."

"Luke, we have to find Copper soon. Look at your crystal," Peter said.

Sure enough, Luke's crystal had turned a shade of gray meaning they had less than an hour. Luke addressed the king. "Do you have any idea where Copper may be?"

The king pulled his beard so hard, Peter thought he'd yank it out. He shook his head, but his wife said, "I heard the men say that the dragon would be dead soon if he didn't agree to help them. The water would surely drown him."

"Ah, that is excellent, Thelia," her husband said. He addressed all his knights. "Where is a place to hide a large dragon, close to the sea with the threat of drowning?"

A younger knight approached the king. "M'lord. I know of such a place. It's where the cliffs hang close together and a ship can barely pass. For months it lays bare so that a person can walk across. But when the seasons change even a ship cannot get through."

"That must be it!" the king said and hoped it was true. They needed to reunite Copper with his family.

After much deliberating, the plan was to take the king and queen plus two of their knights. They figured the dragons could handle two passengers.

As they prepared, Norris snorted and Luke bent his head

toward his companion. Then lifted his head and laughed. "You are confident! I'll give you that!"

"What is so funny?" Rose wanted to know.

"Norris is insulted. He says he can carry at least three people without a problem, so I agreed."

The other dragons wanted to try also, but Norris bellowed to them and they stopped.

"You are all strong and brave. Your father will be very proud when he gets to meet you. Now is everyone ready? We don't have much time," Luke mind-spoke to the dragons.

He explained to the king and queen about their time restraint. The king accepted his explanation without question. Norris moved a boulder in front of the hole, so that their escape would go unnoticed.

The cliffs appeared within minutes of their departure. "Won't Copper be guarded?" Rose asked the queen who was hanging on behind her.

"It is a chance we must take, but if the tide is coming in there will not be much room for another dragon and man to stand watch," she replied.

Rose could see where Meriwether had gotten her beauty. Her mother's hair was long and dark like her daughter's, and although her purple dress was ripped and dirty she wore it regally.

Finder bellowed and pointed his trunk toward the cliffs. "He must see something," Rose said.

"Look!" Peter yelled. "It's Copper!"

As they flew closer, they could see an enormous dragon covered by nets, which were attached to the cliff.

Queen Thelia was right in that there wasn't a great deal of room, but they all managed to land in front of Copper, who had been bellowing and shooting fire toward them.

"Copper!" King Alfred called out. The dragon stopped and snorted in despair.

"He's magnificent!" Rose said hopping off of Sparkle. Finder wiggled to get free and ran off.

"He's gigantic! Twice the size of Shimmer!" Peter said.

When Copper saw the dragons, his hooded eyes widened in surprise, and he pulled and shook at his netted prison. Norris pumped on his chest and with his front claws attempted to rip the net in half. It didn't budge. Boulder ran into it, but fell back. Patch and Sparkle stood still and stared at their enormous father.

King Alfred touched the material on the net and said, "It's like a thick coat of chain mail. How will we release him without swords?"

Luke and Mark pulled on the net. "It looks like a bunch of metal wire wrapped together like on a bridge," Mark said. "How did they know how to build this?"

Rolling two gold balls in his hand that he had grabbed from the volcano, Luke answered, "I don't know, but it does raise some questions like who would have this technology." Pulling on the netting again, he asked, "Mark, can you draw some heavy duty wire cutters or something that will cut steel?"

"Sure, let's try industrial wire cutters first. These are thick, but maybe it'll work."

As Mark started to draw, Finder tooted and grabbed Luke's leg. "What's up, little buddy? You want me to follow you?"

Luke walked around Copper and into a shallow cave. He turned on his flashlight and shown the beam along the wall. He heard a noise like sniffling and picked up his pace when Finder took off. "Hold on, Finder!"

As Luke came around a turn, he tripped when he saw a girl hanging from the wall with her arms extended over her head. Her hair covered her face, but he could tell that she was young and tiny. She shimmered like the ocean on a sunny day. Her head hung limp, so Luke stepped closer. "Hello? I'm a friend. Don't be afraid. We've come to save Copper, so we can save you, too."

She slowly lifted her head, and Luke's world exploded. Even her blue eyes shimmered; her hair was beautiful despite the fact that it was the color of seaweed—black and green with a hint of dark blue. "I have been waiting for you and accept your help."

Luke fished in his pocket and pulled out his Swiss army knife, ever thankful that his dad gave it to him for his birthday. Luke sawed through the rope, trying not to pull too hard since she grimaced every time her arm moved. "What's your name?" he asked wanting to distract her.

"Natalia."

"Beautiful name. I'm Luke."

Her arm fell limp to her side, and Luke caught her just as she was about to slam into the wall. With one arm, Luke held her and sawed with the other. Finder jumped onto his shoulder and nibbled at the rope, too.

"Good boy. Almost there."

The rope gave, and Luke easily picked up Natalia. He pocketed his knife and carried her out of the cave.

Peter ran to his brother. "What happened? Who is that? Is she all right? I was worried you disappeared! Don't do that!" Tears formed in Peter's eyes, and he quickly blinked them away.

"I'm here, Peter. This is Natalia."

Peter took Natalia's legs and then placed her on the sand near everyone else.

"Where did she come from?" Rose asked.

"Finder found her in the cave. She was held prisoner, too."

Copper mind-spoke to Luke. "Copper said that she is from the city of Atlantis and was taken by Lord Tam to be ransomed. He is one greedy man."

"Like the lost city of Atlantis?" Rose asked.

"I'm not sure," Luke answered.

"We're ready, Luke," Mark said.

"Stay with her, will you Rose?"

Rose nodded. Luke walked over to the net where Mark held an oversized wire cutter. Luke handed it to one of the bigger knights who would probably be able to cut faster than either he or Mark.

Starting at the bottom of the net, he pressed the handle together and, with a great deal of effort, cut the wire.

"Yes!" Mark said and pumped his fist in the air. Everyone cheered and the knight, whose name was Claudius snipped the next wire until he had made a small opening.

"You'll have to climb up the net to make the hole bigger for Copper," Luke said.

Copper was soon able to fold in his wings and step out of the net. He shot into the sky watching for any other dragons coming their way, which would signal that the enemy was returning. Without warning, Norris, Boulder, Patch, and Sparkle flew after their father and put on an aerial display. The kids laughed and as they landed, Luke announced it was time to go.

He knelt by Natalia and she grasped his hand. "You stay," she said.

"But, this isn't my home and if I stay, I can never go

back," Luke started.

"This is your place," Natalia insisted.

Rose's face reddened, and she clenched her fists together. This girl was too rude. She didn't even know Luke. "He's our friend and is coming back with us."

"Luke we need to go," Mark said getting nervous as he watched Luke's crystal get darker.

King Alfred knelt down by the girl. "We shall take care of her. You go and meet us at the Great Gathering. We will combine forces with neighboring kingdoms to rid the land of Tam once and for all. He has caused enough trouble. You meet us there when you can return."

Luke nodded and stood. Peter had grabbed the puzzle and opened it on the ground. As the four of them touched the puzzle, Natalia lurched forward and grabbed Luke's arm. He was momentarily caught between their two worlds.

They fell onto the basement floor. Luke followed a moment after, but didn't respond when they shook him.

"Oh no! Is he stuck there again?" Rose asked, frantically wringing her hands together.

Mark knelt over Luke and whispered in his ear. "Luke. Come on. We need you here. Come back to us."

Luke's eyes fluttered open, and he smiled at his best friend. "I'm here, Mark."

Mark helped Luke sit up, and that's when they noticed Peter on the floor with his knees curled up to his chest and his face hidden in his arms. Luke sat down and wrapped his little brother in his arms. "It's all right, Peter."

Rose began to cry as she sat on the other side of Peter and hugged him. She said, "Maybe we shouldn't go back. I'm getting a very bad feeling."

Mark sat next to his sister and put his arm around her.

He said, "Somehow I don't think we have a choice." He could tell by Luke's expression that he agreed. Sometimes a wish can be granted, but not how someone might want it.

The kids had been so caught up with Shimmer's world and the battle against Lord Tam that they almost forgot about the party for Luke. Instructor Adam and his wife, Isilda, wanted to get everyone together to support Luke and his family. Luke and Peter's aunts and uncles came, as well as their cousins, and friends from karate and school.

The theme was a Hawaiian luau with tiki torches, grass skirts, leis, and a pig roasting on an open pit. When Luke first became ill and couldn't swim and run around, all his friends started playing poker. As the sun set behind the tall pine trees, lights glowed on the back porch. Luke and the closest people he knew sat around the table playing for M & M's. Luke was exhausted, but he didn't want this day to end. He carefully studied everyone as they placed their bets. He loved them all and hoped they knew he always would. Luke told some jokes and everyone laughed. When the game ended, he entertained both kids and adults with his magic tricks.

The next day Luke had to go to the hospital to get more medicine. He hoped he would start to feel better. The only time he did now was when he was with the dragons. Luke pondered that thought and wondered why traveling to this other realm made such a difference. He wouldn't mind going back and forth except it didn't make him feel any better here. Luke thought he heard Norris calling his name, but as he fell asleep he realized that it was Natalia, the mermaid calling to him; calling him home.

"We've got to get back to the Great Gathering and bring

Luke with us," Peter whispered as he sat with Rose and Mark in their backyard. Peter was staying at his friends' house while his parents were with Luke at the hospital. Rachel interrupted their conversation to say that they needed to get down to the hospital right away. No one asked questions, because no one wanted any answers. Peter grabbed his backpack with the puzzle and Luke's crystal in it. Luke didn't want to take a chance losing the crystal, so he had given it to Peter to hold.

The long corridor to Luke's room felt like a mile to Peter. Nurses who usually smiled looked like they had been crying, and Peter felt uncomfortable when they touched his hair and patted his shoulder. Peter didn't want to be touched. He wanted his family. Rachel and Sam walked into the room first. Then they brought in the kids. The room was very dim. Luke was asleep on the bed. Rose nudged Peter and after the nurse finished checking Luke, Peter asked if he, Rose, and Mark could have a few minutes alone with Luke. His mom hugged him and everyone left.

Mark and Peter moved in slow motion so Rose took over.

"We have to do this quick," Rose said. "Give me his crystal." Peter handed it to her. "Lift his head. Gently now."

Mark lifted Luke while Rose placed the crystal around his neck. They opened the puzzle, lay it on the portable stand, and moved it next to Luke. Rose held Luke's hand on the puzzle and as everyone else placed their hands next to his, Peter slid in the final piece.

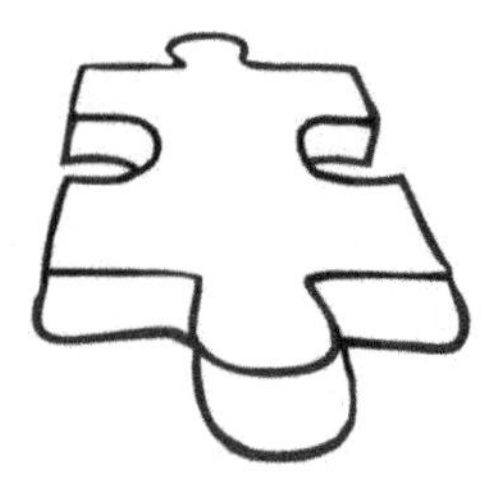

Chapter Fourteen

They fell in a pile of hay and rolled onto a dirt floor. It was dark in the barn, but they could hear music and people laughing and singing. Natalia was waiting for them and as Luke faded in and out, she placed her hand on his arm until he fully appeared. He smiled at her, and everyone spoke at once as they hugged Luke.

"Hold up, everyone," Luke said lifting his hands to fend off all the questions. "I'm not sure what happened. I fell asleep and dreamt of Natalia, and we went for a walk to some silver castle under the water. I couldn't get back."

"What does she have to do with anything?" Rose asked not trying to keep the rudeness out of her voice.

Luke smiled. He always loved Rose's ferocity when it came to protecting those she loved. "I appreciate your concern, Rose, but I think Natalia was trying to protect me."

Natalia nodded. "Luke is between worlds. I only helped him to be in the one where he feels better. He is better here, yes?"

"You're very ill at home, Luke. But I'm happy you are fine now. Maybe once this quest is over, we'll get our wish and you will be healthy again," Peter said.

"Yeah, and I'll kick your butt!" Luke said, grabbing his little brother and giving him a noogie.

"I think we'd better get out there and find the king," Mark said, very solemn.

Luke slapped Mark on this shoulder and said, "You're right, Mark. I can always count on you to keep us on track."

They opened the barn door and followed the music. The Great Gathering had begun. There seemed to be hundreds of people stretched for miles. Some danced to the beat of the fastest drums Luke had ever heard. Others ate chunks of meat with their hands that he could see were cut right off the spit. It reminded Luke of his pig roast. He laughed thinking about how similar it was. As they approached the dancing, he noticed King Alfred and a group of warriors deep in conversation around a large fire. Luke cleared his throat and everyone looked at him. "Ah! There you are! Come sit," said King Alfred. He addressed the other men. "These are the young warriors I have told you about. They will help us defeat Tam once and for all."

Once again they were forced to deal with doubtful stares. Luke wasn't in the mood to prove their worth so he got right to the point.

"What is your plan, King Alfred?"

"Come. Sit and join us," he said. Rose and Peter sat at the base of a tree. Finder hung from his tail off a low branch and sniffed Rose's hair. She gasped and then laughed.

"Down you silly little guy," Rose said opening her arms. Finder dropped into them, and she tickled his belly. Finder wiggled and wrapped his paws around her hair that was the longest it had ever been.

"Why haven't we seen our dragons yet?" Peter whispered to Rose.

"Maybe we can find them after the king is done talking."

Mark and Luke sat on a log to the left of the king. Queen Thelia sat on his right side and stared silently into the fire. Natalia sat next to the queen and whispered something to her. Luke wondered if she worried about Meriwether. He knew that his mom would be out of her mind with worry.

King Alfred began, "We do not know if Tam has invaded my kingdom, so I must assume that he has since there are only a handful of knights and Shimmer left to defend it. It is with great haste that we should leave at sundown. This way we can fly undetected." He paused and stared pointedly at each of the men who shared his fire. "We know that Tam's greed knows no bounds. If he succeeds in forcing my daughter's hand and taking my land, he will continue to the neighboring villages. You know which ones those are and so should be as worried as I am."

Everyone nodded in agreement.

"Then it is decided that we wage war against Tam. Until nightfall, let us eat and enjoy the festivities."

No one seemed concerned about how these warriors would all get to Meriwether in time, so Rose asked, "King Alfred, how will everyone travel to your lands?"

King Alfred stood. "I must beg your forgiveness, Lady Rose. I forget that you are new to our lands and do not know about the other dragons."

"There are more?" asked Peter.

"Yes, there are, but not enough if we want our line of dragons to continue. Certainly there aren't enough if they fight one another. I do not know how many dragons Tam has, but to have the first golden dragon in a century could indeed be our downfall."

Queen Thelia grasped his open hand so he could help

her stand. "I will show you," he said.

Anticipating their reunion with the dragons, Peter could barely keep behind the king. Luke kept placing his hand on his little brother's shoulder to slow him down. Rose was just as excited. She didn't know how many dragons there were, but it was all she could do to not sprint over the hill they were approaching.

The king stopped and said, "Go see for yourself."

Not waiting for their brothers, Rose and Peter raced to the edge. Finder bounced around their legs. They stopped at the edge of a cliff. No words could describe what they saw.

"There must be 20 dragons," Mark said unable to believe that this many dragons existed.

"I don't see our dragons," Rose complained. "Sparkle!" she called.

Luke shut his eyes and pictured Norris. *"Hey, Bud,"* he mind-spoke. *"We're back."*

A loud bellow sounded at the far end of the field and along with their dragons approaching at a rapid speed, a fifth one followed Norris as if she was afraid to lose him.

As usual, Patch landed less than gracefully, Sparkle snorted water all over everyone before they could take cover, and Boulder made a black skid mark across the grass as he landed. Norris circled in the air with the purple-hued dragon nipping at his tail.

Luke laughed and said out loud, "Bring her here, Norris. We'd love to meet her."

Landing with a loud thump, Norris bellowed his greeting to Luke and wrapped him in his wings. Then he bowed his head to the female dragon next to him. Luke responded, "It's nice to meet you, Amaranthine."

"Is she Norris' girlfriend?" Rose asked, loving her brilliantly colored scales. Amaranthine had long eyelashes that she flitted mercilessly at Norris, who responded with pushing his broad chest out even further.

"That's all we need. Norris distracted by a girl dragon," Mark moaned.

"Maybe she's the dragon that I sensed when the eggs hatched," Peter said.

"It's possible, Peter. Norris will fight when needed. Isn't that right?" Luke said hitting his dragon on the chest.

Norris lifted his mouth to the sky and blasted fire while he roared his loyalty to Luke.

"I don't think we'll have to worry about him, and it's nice he has found a friend," Rose said.

They passed the day eating, preparing their weapons and practicing aerial spins on their dragons. It was decided that Natalia would fly behind Luke, and there really wasn't a choice as she seemed as glued to his side as Amaranthine was to Norris'.

When the sun began its descent, an army of dragons and warriors took to the skies to reclaim King Alfred's realm.

It wasn't until they flew over Crystal Lake, in the early morning light, that they heard the clash of swords against shields.

"I hope we're not too late!" Rose cried. Finder lifted his head and wailed at all the noise.

King Alfred organized the dragons in a V formation and, when they could see the castle, had the tail end of the group separate to the left and the right of the castle to cut off the enemy. Trollics attempted to climb the walls of the castle and the few knights left frantically poured hot water over the edge to slow them down. The houses along the base of the castle hill were on fire.

Luke was amazed at the use of wooden catapults and couldn't imagine how they had gotten them half way up the steep hill, but quickly ordered his brother and friends to destroy them before the castle burned down. Some flames could be seen within the castle walls and Rose steered Sparkle over them. Sparkle shot out water like an oversized fire hose and put the fires out. Rose threw her bola knocking the enemies off the castle walls and quickly snapped her fingers so she could throw it again.

As Peter spun Patch down toward the knights firing the catapult, one of them aimed the fiery ball straight at him. Confident in Boulder's ability to know where help was needed, Mark had anticipated needing protection. With no time to spare, an enormous shield formed in front of Peter and Patch, protecting them from the ball of flames. Patch dropped straight down and swiped the knights and their weapons with his tail. They fell into the water, not able to get out.

"Woohoo!" Peter yelled and spun back into the sky.

"Nice team work!" Luke called.

With so many dragons, most of the enemy on the ground had either surrendered or were eliminated. Luke had just turned Norris to face a group of knights when he felt heat sear across his back. Norris bellowed, shot up into the sky, and turned to face their attacker.

"Well, well, well," Lord Tam sneered. "I didn't expect a group of children to be able to launch an attack. It is desperate times indeed when the king has to hire would-be knights."

Lord Tam sat astride the golden dragon, Cíartan. Cíartan's eyes glowed blood red, and the sun glinted off his golden scales. He was larger than Norris and black, acrid smoke billowed from his nostrils.

Sweat ran down Luke's back as he wondered how he would defeat such an angry beast. Everything about the dragon felt evil, but Luke couldn't help but think that it was Lord Tam's taint that affected it. There had to be some good left. Luke thought about what or who could bring out goodness in someone. He thought of his mom and how much she gave to others, and how every day after school she hugged both him and Peter and made them feel like they were the most important people in the world. To her, they probably were. Luke didn't want to think about what his mom would do without him, but he couldn't go there yet. He knew what he had to do.

Settling his mind, he mind-spoke to Shimmer, *"Cíartan is here. Come save your dragon."* He hadn't seen Shimmer since their fighting began, and he tried not to think the worst. Some of the older dragons that long ago shunned Shimmer and Copper had asked for Copper's forgiveness. He gave it. Surely a young dragon could change if these older dragons did. Luke felt Shimmer and moments later, the motherly yet powerful dragon appeared behind Cíartan with Meriwether on her back.

Sensing someone behind him, Cíartan flipped around and a mocking smile crossed Lord Tam's face. "Princess Meriwether. Do you come to surrender and present yourself as my bride?"

Meriwether didn't bother hiding the disgust on her face. "Lord Tam. I'd rather kiss one of your trollics than marry you."

Lord Tam's face ignited into a flood of fury. "That can be arranged!" he sputtered. "But first I will destroy all that you hold dear and that includes that dragon of yours!"

Shimmer watched Cíartan and searched for the glimmer of recognition that day he hatched. She mind-spoke to him, *"If you attack me, then all you do from this day forward will be tainted with evil and greed. Our kind was raised to help others and keep magic in our world. Come back to me."*

Cíartan's eyes had turned the color of the blackest night when Lord Tam had bonded with him. Now there were flecks of gold trying to flash through. Filled with hope, Shimmer was surprised when Lord Tam produced a spear and aimed it toward Shimmer's heart. If her child would turn evil, Shimmer wasn't sure she wanted to be here to see it.

Just then Patch flew in and circled over and under Cíartan throwing him off guard. Sparkle squirted water at Lord Tam, which gave time for Rose to throw her bola at his arm. It connected and knocked the spear out of his hand. Enraged, Lord Tam commanded, "Char these dragons once and for all!"

Cíartan snorted smoke and opened his mouth to spew fire. Mark eased Boulder closer and turned sideways. He spun his Bo staff so fast, a gale of wind blew toward Cíartan, so that instead of exhaling smoke, he inhaled air and choked. Norris wrenched Lord Tam off of Cíartan's back with his claws and dropped him in the deep depths of the water.

Everyone ignored Lord Tam's distant cries for help. They forced Cíartan to the ground and circled him. Amaranthine joined the group, and Shimmer landed facing her lost dragon. Cíartan snorted smoke in defiance. He looked toward the sky as a possible means of escape and finally peered into his mother's eyes. Shimmer held his gaze and her love filled him. Before he could turn away, she completed the bond that had been cut short. Cíartan collapsed to the ground, his eyes closed.

"Oh no!" cried Meriwether jumping off of Shimmer's back. She knelt next to him and rubbed his head. "Come back to us, Cíartan. We know you are meant for goodness."

Rose, Mark, Luke, Peter, and Natalia all placed their hands on Cíartan and encouraged him to wake up. When Cíartan opened his eyes, they shone with the same gold hue as his scales. He nudged Meriwether's tiny hand and stood back on his own hind legs.

Everyone cheered and Cíartan's siblings proceeded to wrestle with him in welcome. They each held their brother's gaze so that the familial bond was almost complete. Not knowing Amaranthine's family, Shimmer asked if she would like to be a part of their family. When she agreed Shimmer bonded with the purple-hued dragon and welcomed her to the family. Over 20 dragons and their riders had amassed on the fields to help King Alfred regain his throne.

A roar sounded from the center of the dragons, and Shimmer left her dragons to play while she searched for Copper. He wasn't hard to find as the sun glinted off his copper scales, and he towered over the other dragons. Spreading his wings much like Norris always did, Shimmer bent her head and leaned on her mate. Copper enfolded her in his wings and a sigh of relief shuddered through them both. Then six young dragons flew into the sky roaring their triumph while their riders hooted in delight. Finally, they landed in front of Copper and Shimmer. Copper bonded with his children, and the family was complete.

"Together at last," Meriwether said. She then ran to her mother and father and cried in their arms, the need to be their child overruling her months of being a leader.

"Meriwether," her mother exclaimed. "I knew that we would see you again, but what a warrior you have become!"

Meriwether laughed through her tears. "I am not a warrior, Mother, but I knew where to find the ones we needed."

"A true warrior knows her strengths and finds others to fill her weaknesses. It seems you have done that, and we owe you a great debt of gratitude," her father said.

"Having you all back is gratitude enough," Meriwether said.

When the trollics and warriors had seen Lord Tam fall from his dragon, they raced back into the forest. King Alfred's most trusted knights fished Tam out of the water. His angry eyes flashed and he roared, "This is not the end! You think I am the only enemy?"

King Alfred silenced him and took the leather necklace from around Tam's neck. It held a lock of Meriwether's hair that had been used to keep her trapped on her land. King Alfred withdrew her hair and let it blow away into the wind. "My daughter is no longer trapped by your childish wizardry. You are hereby banned from Dragonia or any land surrounding it."

Tam continued, "These children will be your downfall! One such as them will destroy you!"

Placed in chains, Tam was tied to a tree at the base of the castle. No one wanted his evilness to taint the castle.

"What did he mean by those words? What other enemy is there?" Meriwether asked her father.

"I do not know, but it is not the time to question him."

Now that Copper and Cíartan were safe with their family, and her parents had returned, Meriwether called Luke, Mark, Rose, and Peter to her. Without a word, she placed her hands on their cheeks and kissed each one. Peter's face turned bright red, Rose remembered every movement so she could act just like Meriwether when she was home, Mark looked down at the ground, and Luke beamed. "Will you introduce me to your friend, Sir Luke?" Meriwether asked pointing to Natalia.

Luke cleared his throat and said, "Princess Meriwether. I'd like to introduce Natalia of Atlantis."

Meriwether's eyes shot open, and she nodded as if understanding why Natalia was with them. "I see that you are far from home as my family was, Princess Natalia. Perhaps some brave knights will take you back."

"This is so, but Tam left evil at my home. There is great magic here, and I hope you will help us when the time comes. I am grateful to you for saving me," she said as she took Luke's hand.

This time it was Luke's face that turned red with embarrassment.

Rose giggled, and Peter joined in putting his finger in his mouth like he was gagging.

"Enough, you two," Mark warned.

Meriwether laughed. "I will miss all of you. You must visit with me during your other adventurous travels."

"We'll be coming back?" Rose asked, hope filling her eyes.

Meriwether glanced at Luke like she was going to ask a question, but his solemn face told her that he hadn't said anything to his brother or his friends yet. *All in its own time,* she thought.

"Of course! That crystal will take you wherever you are most needed, and I have a feeling there are many adventures waiting for you." Peter and Rose hugged each other like they couldn't wait to get started. "But now it is time to revel in our victory and celebrate. I am sure your time is growing short," Meriwether said.

With that, Luke glanced at his crystal and replied, "For some reason it has taken longer to get darker. Maybe the crystal knew we were finishing this quest. We have a couple hours I think. Let's help set up for the party."

Since there were too many dragons and people to fit comfortably in the castle, a celebration was set up in the arena. The fields had been ruined, but time would heal the land, and the people had renewed hope since dragon and man had come together once again. People from the neighboring villages came out of hiding once word had spread that the evil lord had been defeated. Throngs of children came too and soon they were able to act like the kids they were, spinning in circles until they dropped, playing hide and seek amongst the hay bales, and testing their strength arm wrestling. Rose and Natalia didn't participate in that last one, but instead braided each other's hair and spoke of their homes.

"You will visit me, I know," Natalia said with surety.

"How do you know?" Rose asked.

"An enemy threatens my home. Besides, you will all want to be together again."

Rose finished a braid then moved in front of Natalia so she could see her face. "Why wouldn't I see the boys again? I live with one of them and am practically family with Peter and Luke."

"Is Luke well in your world?"

Rose's bright cheeks went pale. "What does that have to do with anything? We finished the quest so he is supposed to get better."

"Answer me."

Rose watched the boys tossing bales of hay to see who

could throw them the farthest. Without a doubt Luke was the strongest, but he was very athletic so it would make sense. Then an image of Luke lying so skinny and pale in the hospital cut into the happy moment and Rose gasped. Her eyes filled with tears. "No. The deal was that if we finished the quest, Luke would get better," she said.

Natalia took Rose's hand and said, "I will take good care of him. I swear."

Rose pulled her hand away and ran to her brother. She grasped Mark around his back, and he stiffened thinking they were under attack. When he saw his sister crying, he pulled her around and held onto her arms. "What's wrong, Rose? Who made you cry?"

Natalia calmly walked toward them. "I did, and I wish I could take back my words, but they ring true." Catching Luke staring at her, she nodded. "It is time. You must tell them."

"Easy for you to say," Luke mumbled then motioned for everyone to sit on a log by a warm pit, crackling with fire.

"What do you need to tell us, Luke?" Mark asked.

With the excitement of the battle and the celebration after, Luke hadn't thought about the words he would have to say to his best friends and his brother. How could he tell them that he was going away? He had to tell them, but it was so important they know more than that. They had to know he wasn't going away forever like people always said when someone died. He knew so much more now and perhaps that was why he wasn't afraid. He was more afraid, no really just sad, for his family who would have a hard time understanding or believing that he was right there with them in another realm. A realm he now knew was truly as thin as an oak leaf and as durable as the oak tree.

"I have to stay here. I'm not well enough to live with you anymore. That's why we found the portal in the puzzle. It was a test to see if it was time for me to be a part of this world." He looked at Peter. "Kind of like a video game. We can't get to the next level until we prove we have mastered our current level. I did that. Actually we all did that, so you get to move on with me, but in a different way."

Peter stood hands clenched at his sides. "What about our wish? We completed our end of the bargain, and we all wished for you to be healthy! Meriwether lied!"

"Peter, come here."

When Peter didn't move, Luke went to him and wrapped his arm around his little brother.

Rose held onto Finder who had been foraging, but seemed to know when she needed him most. "Are you dying?" she asked.

Peter shook in Luke's arm with both shock and anger. Luke had to get this right. "In a way. I'm dying in the sense that I won't be able to physically be back home." At Rose's cry, Luke leaned forward and took her hand. "We all wished for me to be healthy, but you saw how unhealthy I was at home. I know this is hard. You won't see me there anymore, but you can see me here on your next quest."

He sat back and looked at Mark who had been drawing in his sketchbook since Luke had begun talking. Luke never minded, because he knew Mark listened best with his pencil connected to paper. Next, he studied Peter who had fallen back on his butt and rested his head on his knees. "Peter, can you look at me?"

Peter shook his head, and Luke saw the tears spray left and right. "Peter."

He stared with eyes filled with so much pain, Luke

would have done anything at that moment to be able to go home with him. But he had to be content knowing they would still be together; he only had to prove to them that it was true.

At that moment, Meriwether came over with their dragons and Shimmer. It seemed appropriate that they should all be together encircling one another in love and comfort.

"I know this is difficult for you to understand and accept. You came to me thinking you were going on a quest in exchange for a wish. But you always believed you'd all go home. I had thought so too, until I saw there was another reason I met you. You are worthy knights and faithful friends. Your love has no boundaries. You may see Sir Luke and your dragons, and another quest will come your way, when you are ready. You will always be knights and that means you must always be brave," Meriwether said. Knowing it was time to go, she stood and said, "Now it is time to say goodbye."

Everyone stood as if in a daze.

Luke firmly grasped Peter's shoulders forcing his little brother to look at him.

"I am always a part of you and a puzzle piece away. You'll know when it's time to come. And I will always be there for you. Please trust me on this."

Trying hard not to cry, Peter nodded.

"One more thing." Luke dug into his pocket and handed Peter his *Pokemon Pikachu* figurine.

Peter lifted his hands in protest and said, "No, Luke. I can't."

Luke placed the little yellow character with the red dots on its cheeks in Peter's hand and closed it tight. "A connection you might say. Tell Mom and Dad the story of our great adventure. They will need it. Mark and Rose will help you. After all we know from Mom that a good story has the power to heal."

Luke walked his brother to the puzzle that pictured their basement. He hugged Rose and kissed her on the cheek. He removed his swim goggles from his bag and placed them in her hand. He held hers with both of his. "I'll be watching you swim."

"You knew you weren't coming back with us," Rose said, tears flowing down her pale cheeks.

Finder clung on her back, and he whined because Rose was so sad. He snorted and sniffed her hair. Knowing she couldn't take Finder with her, Rose pulled him around and hugged him. Then she approached Natalia and asked, "Will you keep an eye on Finder while I'm gone?"

Natalia bowed with a smile and said, "Of course." She took Finder from Rose and gave him a hug.

Clasping hands with Mark, Luke pulled him into a bear hug and whispered, "Look out for my little bro. I'm close by, but it will be harder for all of you." To Mark, he handed a pocket-sized book of the cartoons that he and Mark had drawn and written together. "You keep this for me and keep drawing. I'll write the stories the next time I see you. We can switch each time we see one another."

Mark laughed and sobbed at the same time. "Yeah, I like that idea." He handed Luke a folded piece of paper. Luke opened it and there was a drawing of the four of them on the back of their dragons with their thumbs pointed toward the sky. Their smiles captured the magic and love they would always share.

Luke laughed despite the pain he felt in his heart. "Thanks, Mark. For everything." Removing the crystal that connected his world to this enchanted place, Luke walked over to Peter and placed it over his head. "This is yours now. Protect it, and you will always have a way back. Take care of Mom and Dad for me."

Peter nodded, unable to form words.

Natalia slipped her other arm around Luke's waist, silently supporting him as he said goodbye to his family.

"Now go. It's time."

Peter peered down and saw that the crystal was darker. He, Mark, and Rose touched the puzzle. Waving, they traveled back to their home, where they would wait for the next adventure that would bring them back to Luke.

Acknowledgments

This book could not have happened without the many adventures of Nick, Stephen, Emily, and Tyler. I am so grateful I recorded all your many years together. To Karen Patchell for reading through the multiple drafts and to her and Mark, for sharing their family with mine. To the Marsal family for building community through martial arts and their pig roasts.

Special thanks to my talented young readers who taught me so much about writing: Conge L., Ryan D., Christian F., Christopher S., Kolbe L., Ryan C., Bella and Maddie S., Mackenzie and Rebecca H., Patrick M. and Marcy Philo's fourth grade class!

Thank you to Melinda Taormina and Barbara Reese from the Clifton Park-Halfmoon Public Library, who edited my manuscript and added age appropriate insights. I appreciate all the input and encouragement from my Super Cool Writer's Group! For Kathy Lange-Madden for your review and constant support. I appreciate everyone who gave me feedback on the cover, interior, and overall concept. Thank you to Carol Coogan for envisioning the cover and being spot on, as well as the book layout.

Huge thank you to my husband, Lucas, who has encouraged me through each of my books and told me to write because I had important messages to share.

Biography

Janine De Tillio Cammarata has always loved tales of dragons and time travel. When her children were younger, she often made up her own stories as she rocked them to sleep. Now she teaches children and adults to write their own adventures. When she isn't writing or teaching, she is walking her dogs, riding her motorcycle, and helping children battle cancer through her foundation, Nick's Fight to be Healed. She and her family live in Clifton Park, NY. For more information, visit www.fighttobehealed.org.

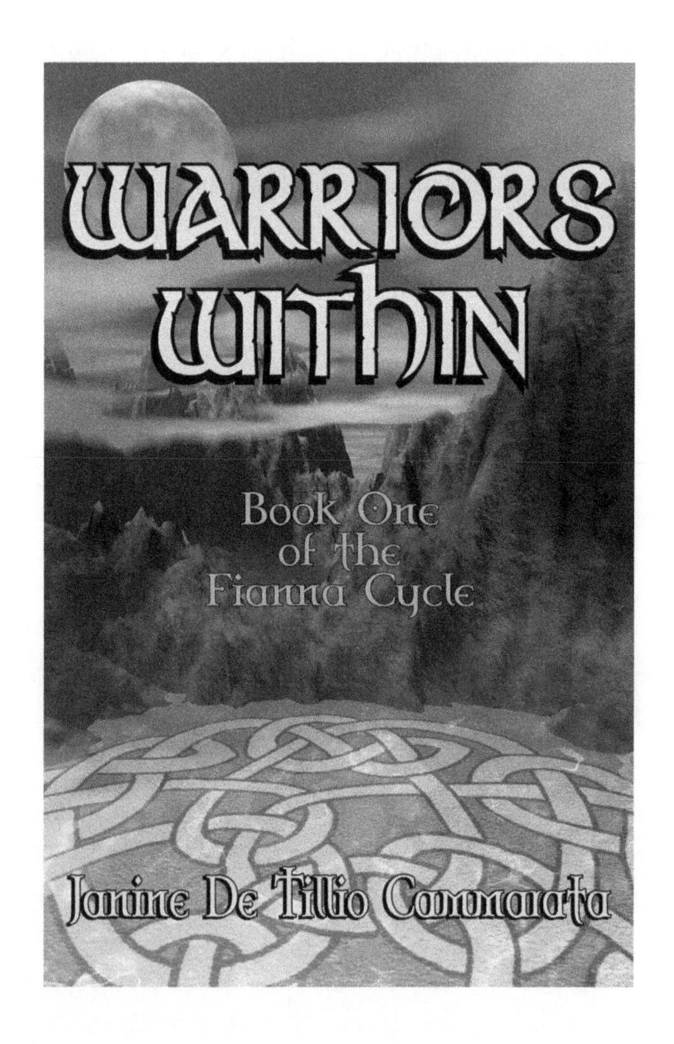
WARRIORS
WITHIN
Book One
of the
Fianna Cycle
Janine De Tillio Cammarata

EYES
OF THE
GODDESS
Book Two
of the
Fianna Cycle
Janine De Tillio Cammarata

What Makes Them Amazing
Inspiring Stories of Young Adults Fighting Cancer
Janine DeTillio Cammarata